PENGUIN CRIME FICTION

Editor: Julian Symons

THE PUSHER

Ed McBain is the pseudonym of Evan Hunter, one of America's most distinguished novelists. After war service in the U.S. Navy, he attended Hunter College, moving from there through teaching and work for a literary agency to become the full-time professional writer he is today. As Ed McBain he has published thirty-one 87th Precinct mysteries which, combined with novels written under his real name, such as the best-selling *Blackboard Jungle*, have sold more than fifty-three million copies worldwide. Evan Hunter lives in a big rambling old house in Connecticut, but never strays for very long from New York City where he was born, and from where he takes the background of his stories.

D0869194

ED McBAIN

THE PUSHER

PENGUIN BOOKS

Penguin Books Ltd, Harmondsworth, Middlesex, England
Penguin Books, 625 Madison Avenue, New York, New York 10022, U.S.A.
Penguin Books Australia Ltd, Ringwood, Victoria, Australia
Penguin Books Canada Ltd, 2801 John Street, Markham, Ontario, Canada L3R 1B4
Penguin Books (N.Z.) Ltd, 182–190 Wairau Road, Auckland 10, New Zealand

—

First published in the U.S.A. 1956
First published in Great Britain by T. V. Boardman 1959
Published in Penguin Books 1963
Reprinted 1964, 1970, 1977, 1978

—

—

Made and printed in Great Britain by
Hazell Watson & Viney Ltd,
Aylesbury, Bucks
Set in Linotype Times

This is for Evelyn and Dick

The city in these pages is imaginary. The people, the places are all fictitious. Only the police routine is based on established investigatory technique.

CHAPTER ONE

WINTER came in like an anarchist with a bomb.

Wild-eyed, shrieking, puffing hard, it caught the city in cold, froze the marrow and froze the heart.

The wind roared under eaves and tore around corners, lifting hats and lifting skirts, caressing warm thighs with icy-cold fingers. The citizens blew on their hands and lifted their coat collars and tightened their mufflers. They had been enmeshed in the slow-dying lethargy of autumn, and now winter was upon them, rapping their teeth with knuckles of ice. The citizens grinned into the wind, but the wind was not in a smiling mood. The wind roared and bellowed, and snow spilled from the skies. covered the city with white and then, muddied and dirtied, yielded to the wind and the cold and turned to treacherous ice.

The citizens deserted the streets. They sought pot-bellied stoves and hissing radiators. They drank cheap rye or expensive Scotch. They crawled under the covers alone, or they found the warmth of another body in the primitive ritual of love while the wind howled outside.

Winter was going to be a bitch this year.

The patrolman's name was Dick Genero, and he was cold. He didn't like winter, and that was that. You could sell him ice skating and skiing and bobsledding and hot rum toddies and all the other fictions of a happy, happy snowy season and he would still tell you to go drop dead someplace. Summer was Genero's season. He was one of those people, that's all. He liked warm sand and a hot sun and blue skies with hardly any clouds in them, and he also liked summer storms with lots of lightning, and he liked flowers blooming and gin-tonics and you could take all the winters that ever were and stuff them into a beat-up old tin can and dump them in the River Dix and Genero would have been a very happy man.

His ears were cold.

'When your ears are cold, you're cold all over,' Genero's mother used to say, and Genero's mother was a well of wisdom on weather conditions. Genero walked his beat with his cold ears, and he thought of his mother, and then unrelatedly and belatedly thought of his wife and wished he were home with her in bed. It was two o'clock in the morning, and any man in his right mind would not be walking the streets of the city at two in the morning with the temperature in the low twenties and a pretty woman at home in bed.

The wind ripped at his winter overcoat, pierced the heavy blue material, and licked at his winter blouse. The cold soaked into his undershirt, and Genero shivered and thought of his ears, remembering not to touch them because if you touched them when they were cold, they would fall off. His mother had told him that, too. He had been tempted on several occasions in his life to touch his ears when they were cold, just to see if they *would* fall off. He was, in truth, afraid they would not – and there would go a son's faith in his mom. So he dutifully kept his gloved hands away from his head, and he ducked his head against the wind and thought of Rosalie home in bed, and thought of Florida and Puerto Rico and the Virgin Isles and Africa, working his way south until he realized abruptly he had reached the South Pole, where the cold still persisted.

It's warm, he told himself. *Come on, now – it's warm.*

Look at all the bathing beauties in their scanty suits. Jesus, but this sand is hot today. Listen to that ocean, ah, thank God for the cool breeze, we can certainly use a cool breeze on a scorcher like today, that's for sure. And . . .

And I'll bet maybe they will fall off if I touch them.

The streets were empty. Well sure, that figured. Only idiots and cops were out tonight. He walked to the candy store and automatically tried the doorknob, cursing the proprietor for not having the store open so that a cop with his ears ready to fall off could go in and have a cup of coffee. Ingrates, he thought, all ingrates. Home and asleep while I'm trying the stupid doorknob. Who'd pull a burglary on a night like this, anyway? A man's fingers would freeze solid to the burglar's tools, the way fingers freeze solid to metal in the Arctic. There's a cheerful thought. Jesus, *I am cold*!

He started up the street. Lanny's Bar was probably still open. He would stop there to see that no fights were in progress and perhaps sneak an against-regulations nip to take the edge off this cold. He could see nothing wrong with a little nip. A man could pretend he was chilly, true, but when a man's underwear showed the ability to stand unaided and independently in the middle of the street, it was time to dispense with the 'chilly' fantasy and realize that freezing was but a stone's throw away. Genero clapped his gloved hands together and lifted his head.

He saw the light.

It came from somewhere up the street. The street was black except for the light. Genero stopped and squinted his eyes against the wind. *The tailor shop*, he thought instantly. That stupid ass Cohen is pressing clothes in the wee hours of the morn again. He would have to warn him. 'Max,' he would have to say, 'you're a hell of a nice guy, but when you're going to be pressing late at night, give the house a ring and wise up us poor bastards, will you?'

Then Max would nod and smile and give him a glass of that sweet wine he kept behind the counter. All at once, Max didn't seem so stupid.

Max was the kind benefactor of all cops walking beats everywhere. Max's light was a shining beacon, the shop a sanctuary for ice-bound freighters. *Get the bottle out, Max*, Genero thought. *I'm on my way.*

He headed for the tailor shop and the light, and he would have really enjoyed that glass of wine with Max, were it not for one thing:

The light was not coming from the tailor shop.

The light came from farther up the street, spilling from the open mouth of the basement steps under one of the tenements. For a moment, Genero was puzzled. If not Max ...

Genero quickened his step. Quite unconsciously, he drew off his right glove and yanked his service revolver from its holster. The faces of the buildings were closed with sleep. Only the light pierced the darkness, and he approached the light warily, stopping before the steps where they descended beyond the hanging chain to enter the bowels of the tenement.

A door was hooded in shadow beneath the brick stoop of the

9

building, and a window was set high up in the brick alongside the door. The window was caked with grime, but it glowed like a single wakeful eye. Cautiously, Genero climbed over the chain and started down the steps.

A narrow alley ran straight as an arrow to the back yard of the tenement. The garbage cans were in for the night, stacked haphazardly in the alleyway, dispelling their stench on the crisp December air. Genero glanced quickly up the alleyway, and then walked quietly to the door.

He stood listening. There was no sound from beyond the door. He held the revolver ready in his right hand, and with his left hand, he twisted the doorknob.

Surprisingly, the door swung open.

Genero backed away suddenly. He was sweating. His ears were still cold, but he was sweating. He listened to the sound of his own breathing, listened for other sounds in the cold sleeping city, listened for the silent scrape of a foot, something, anything. He listened for a long time, and then he entered the basement room.

The light came from a naked bulb suspended from a thick wire cord. It hung absolutely motionless. It did not swing, it did not make the slightest movement, so that the wire cord seemed almost to have been frozen into a slender steel rod. An orange crate rested on the floor beneath the light bulb. There were four bottle caps on the crate. Genero pulled out his pocket flash and swung the arc around the room. There were pin-up pictures on one of the walls, pasted close together, breasts to buttocks, cramped for space. The opposite wall was bare. There was a cot at the far end of the room, and there was a barred window over it.

Genero swung the light a little to the left and then, startled, pulled back, the .38 jerking upward spasmodically.

A boy was sitting on the cot.

His face was blue. He was leaning forward. He was leaning forward at a most precarious angle, and when the first cold shock of discovery left Genero, he wondered why the boy didn't fall forward on to his face. That was when he saw the rope.

One end of the rope was fastened to the barred window.

The other end was knotted around the boy's neck. The boy kept leaning forward expectantly as if he wanted to get up off the cot and break into a sprint. His eyes were wide, and his mouth was open, and there seemed to be life coiled deep within his body, ready to unspring and catapult him into the room. Only the colour of his face and the position of his arms betrayed the fact that he was dead. The blue of the face was a sickly hue; his arms lay like heavy sleepers at his sides, the hands turned palms upward. Several inches from one hand was an empty hypodermic syringe.

Tentatively, somewhat frightened, somewhat ashamed of his superstitious dread of a dead body, Genero took a step closer and studied the blue face in the beam of the flash. To prove he wasn't frightened at all, he stood looking into the blank eyes for a moment or two longer than he felt he had to.

Then he hurried from the room, trembling, and headed for the nearest call box.

CHAPTER TWO

THE word had gone out long before Kling and Carella arrived.

Death had silently invaded the night, and death – like Macbeth – had murdered sleep, and there were lights in the windows now, and people leaned out into the bitter cold of winter, staring down at the five patrolmen who clustered in an uneasy and somehow guilty-looking knot on the pavement. There were people in the streets, too, talking in hushed whispers, wearing overcoats thrown over pyjamas. The Mercury sedan swung into the block, looking like any pleasure car except for the short radio aerial protruding from the centre of the roof. The car carried MD licence plates, but the two men who stepped from it were not doctors; they were detectives.

Carella walked briskly to the patrolmen. He was a tall man, dressed now in a brown sharkskin suit and charcoal-brown overcoat. He was hatless, and his hair was clipped close to his head, and he walked with the athletic nonchalance of a baseball player. He gave an impression of tightness, tight skin drawn taut over hard muscle, tight skin over high cheekbones that gave his face a somewhat Oriental appearance.

'Who called in?' he asked the closest patrolman.

'Dick,' the cop answered.

'Where is he?'

'Downstairs with the stiff.'

'Come on, Bert,' Carella said over his shoulder, and Kling followed obediently and silently. The patrolmen studied Kling with pretended aloofness, not quite able to hide their envy. Kling was a new detective, a twenty-four-year-old kid who'd come up from the ranks. 'Come up,' hell. 'Shot up' was a better way to put it. 'Streaked up' was, in fact, the best way to put it. Kling had cracked a homicide, and the other patrolmen called it dumb luck, but the Commissioner called it 'unusual perceptiveness and tenacity', and since the Commissioner's opinion was somewhat more highly respected than the opinions of beat-walkers, a rookie patrolman had been promoted to 3rd Grade Detective in less time than it took to pronounce the rank.

So the patrolmen smiled bleakly at Kling as he climbed over the chain after Carella, and the greenish tint to their faces was not caused by the cold.

'What's the matter with *him*?' one of the patrolmen whispered. 'Don't he say hello no more?'

If Kling heard him, he gave no sign. He followed Carella into the basement room. Dick Genero was standing under the light bulb, biting his lip.

'Hi, Dick,' Carella said.

'Hello, Steve. Bert.' Genero seemed very nervous.

'Dick,' Kling acknowledged.

'When'd you find him?' Carella asked.

'Few minutes before I called in. He's over there.' Genero did not turn to look at the body.

'You touch anything?'

'Jesus, no!'

'Good. Was he alone when you got here?'

'Yeah. Yeah, he was alone. Listen, Steve, you mind if I go Upstairs for some air? It's a little . . . a little stuffy in here.'

12

'In a minute,' Carella said. 'Was the light burning?'

'What? Oh, yeah. Yeah, it was.' Genero paused. 'That's how I happened to come down. I figured maybe a burglar. When I come down, there he was.' Genero flicked his eyes toward the body on the cot.

Carella walked to where the boy sat suspended by the rope. 'How old can he be?' he asked of no one. 'Fifteen, sixteen?' No one answered.

'It looks . . . it looks like he hung himself, don't it?' Genero asked. Studiously, he avoided looking at the boy.

'It looks that way,' Carella said. He did not realize that he was unconsciously shaking his head, or that there was a pained expression on his face. He sighed and turned to Kling. 'We'd better wait until the Homicide boys get here. They raise a stink if we leave them seconds. What time is it, Bert?'

Kling looked at his watch. 'Two eleven,' he said.

'Want to start keeping a timetable, Dick?'

'Sure,' Genero said. He took a black pad from his hip pocket and began writing into it. Carella watched him.

'Let's go up and get that air,' he said.

Most suicides don't realize the headaches they cause.

They slash their wrists, or turn on the gas jets, or shoot themselves, or bang a slew of parallel wounds into their skulls with a hatchet, or leap from the nearest window, or sometimes chew a little cyanide, or – as seemed to be the case with the boy on the cot – they hang themselves. But they don't give a thought to the headaches of the law enforcers.

A suicide, you see, is initially treated exactly like a homicide. And in a homicide, there are a few people concerned with law enforcement who must be notified. These few people are:

1. The police commissioner.
2. The chief of detectives.
3. The district commander of the detective division.
4. Homicide North or Homicide South, depending upon where the body was found.
5. The squad and precinct commanding officers of the precinct in which the body was found.

6. The medical examiner.
7. The district attorney.
8. The telegraph, telephone, and teletype bureau at head-quarters.
9. The police laboratory.
10. The police photographers.
11. The police stenographers.

Not all of these people, of course, descend simultaneously upon the scene of a suicide. Some of them have no earthly reason for climbing out of bed at an ungodly hour, and some of them simply leave the job to lesser paid and highly trained subordinates. You can always count on a diehard contingent of night owls, however, and this group will include a few Homicide dicks, a photographer, an assistant medical examiner, a handful of patrolmen, a pair or more of dicks from the local precinct, and a few lab technicians. A stenographer may or may not come along for the show.

At 2.11 or thereabouts in the morning, nobody feels much like working.

Oh sure, a corpse breaks up the dull monotony of the midnight tour; and it's nice to renew acquaintances with old friends from Homicide South; and maybe the photographer has a few choice samples of French postcard art to pass around; but all in all, nobody has much heartfelt enthusiasm for a suicide at 2.11. Especially when it's cold.

There was no questioning the fact that it was cold.

The dicks from Homicide South looked as if someone had pulled them from the freezer compartment a few moments before. They walked stiff-legged to the sidewalk, their hands thrust into their coat pockets, their heads bent, their fedoras pulled low over their faces. One lifted his head long enough to say hello to Carella, and then they both followed him and Kling into the basement room.

'Little better down here,' the first cop said. He rubbed his hands together, glanced over at the body, and then said, 'I don't suppose anybody has a flask with him?' He looked at the faces of the other cops. 'No, I didn't suppose so,' he said sourly.

14

'Patrolman named Dick Genero discovered the body at about 2.04,' Carella said. 'The light was burning, and nothing's been touched.'

The first Homicide cop grunted, and then sighed. 'Well, better get to work, huh?' he asked with eager enthusiasm.

The second Homicide cop looked at the body. 'Stupid,' he mumbled. 'Why didn't he wait until morning?' He glanced at Kling. 'Who are you?' he asked.

'Bert Kling,' Kling said, and then – as if the question had been burning his throat since he'd first seen the body – he asked, 'I thought the body had to be swinging free in a hanging suicide.'

The Homicide cop stared at Kling, and then turned to Carella. 'Is this guy a cop?' he asked.

'Sure,' Carella said.

'I thought maybe you brought one of your relatives along for a thrill.' He turned back to Kling. 'No, son,' he said, 'the body don't have to be swinging free. You want proof?' He pointed to the cot. 'There's a hanging suicide, and the body ain't swinging free, now, is it?'

'Well, no, it isn't.'

'You're quite a whiz,' Carella said. He was not smiling. He caught the Homicide cop's eyes and held them.

'I get by,' the Homicide cop said. 'I ain't from the crackerjack 87th Precinct, but I been on the force twenty-two years now, and I've broken up a few ticktacktoe games in my time.'

There was no irony or sarcasm in Carella's voice when he answered. He played it deadpan, apparently serious. 'Men like you are a credit to the force,' he said.

The Homicide cop eyed Carella warily. 'I was only trying to explain. . . .'

'Sure,' Carella said. 'Stupid kid here doesn't realize the body doesn't have to be swinging free. Why, Bert, we've found them standing, sitting, and lying.' He turned to the Homicide cop. 'Isn't that right?'

'Sure, all positions.'

'Sure,' Carella agreed. 'A suicide doesn't have to look like one.' A barely concealed hardness had crept into his voice, and Kling frowned and then glanced somewhat apprehensively

15

toward the Homicide dicks. 'What do you think of the colour?' Carella asked.

The dick who'd blown his top at Carella approached him cautiously. 'What?' he asked.

'The blue. Interesting, isn't it?'

'Cut off the air, you get a blue body,' the Homicide cop answered. 'Simple as all that.'

'Sure,' Carella said, the hardness more apparent in his voice now. 'Very simple. Tell the kid about side knots.'

'What?'

'The knot on the rope. It's on the side of the boy's neck.'

The Homicide cop walked over and looked at the body. 'So what?' he asked.

'I just thought a hanging-suicide expert like yourself might have noticed it,' Carella said, the hardness of his voice completely unmasked now.

'Yeah, I noticed it. So what?'

'I thought you might want to explain to a new detective like the kid here the coloration we sometimes get in hangings.'

'Look, Carella,' the other Homicide cop started.

'Let your pal talk, Fred,' Carella interrupted. 'We don't want to miss the testimony of an expert.'

'What the hell are you talking about?'

'He's needling you, Joe,' Fred said.

Joe turned to Carella. 'You needling me?'

'I wouldn't know how,' Carella said. 'Explain the knot, expert.'

Joe blinked. 'Knot, knot, what the hell are you talking about?'

'Why, surely you know,' Carella said sweetly, 'that a side knot will completely compress the arteries and veins on one side of the neck only.'

'Sure, I know that,' Joe said.

'And you know, of course, that the face will usually be red when the knot's been tied at the side of the neck – as opposed to the face being pale when the knot's tied at the nape. You know that, don't you?'

'Sure, I know that,' Joe said arrogantly. 'And we've had

16

them turn blue in both side-knot and nape-knot cases, so what the hell are you telling me? I've had a dozen blue strangle cases.'

'How many dozen blue cyanide-poisoning cases have you had?'

'Huh?'

'How do you know the cause of death was asphyxiation?'

'Huh?'

'Did you see those burnt bottle caps on the orange crate? Did you see the syringe next to the boy's hand?'

'Sure I did.'

'Do you think he's a junkie?'

'I guess he is. It would be my guess that he is,' Joe said. He paused and made a concerted effort at sarcasm. 'What do the masterminds of the 87th think?'

'I would guess he's an addict,' Carella said, 'judging from the "hit" marks on his arms.'

'I saw his arms, too,' Joe said. He searched within the labyrinthine confines of his intelligence for something further to say, but the something eluded him.

'Do you suppose the kid shot up before he hanged himself?' Carella asked sweetly.

'He might have,' Joe said judiciously.

'Be a little confusing if he did, wouldn't it?' Carella asked.

'How so?' Joe said, rushing in where angels might have exercised a bit of caution.

'If he'd just had a fix, he'd be pretty happy. I wonder why he'd take his own life.'

'Some junkies get morose,' Fred said. 'Listen, Carella, lay off. What the hell are you trying to prove, anyway?'

'Only that the masterminds of the 87th don't go yelling suicide until we've seen an autopsy report – and maybe not even then. How about that, Joe? Or do *all* blue bodies automatically mean strangulation?'

'You got to weigh the facts,' Joe said. 'You got to put them all together.'

'There's a shrewd observation on the art of detection, Bert,' Carella said. 'Mark it well.'

'Where the hell are the photographers?' Fred said, tired of

the banter. 'I want to get started on the body, find out who the hell the kid is, at least.'

'He's in no hurry,' Carella said.

CHAPTER THREE

THE boy's name was Aníbal Hernandez. The kids who weren't Puerto Rican called him Annabelle. His mother called him Aníbal, and she pronounced the name with Spanish grandeur, but the grandeur was limp with grief.

Carella and Kling had trekked the five flights to the top floor of the tenement and knocked on the door of apartment fifty-five. She had opened the door quickly, as if knowing that visitors would soon be calling. She was a big woman with ample breasts and straight black hair. She wore a simple dress, and there was no make-up on her face, and her cheeks were streaked with tears.

'Police?' she asked.

'Yes,' Carella said.

'Come in, *por favor*. Please.'

The apartment was very still. Nothing broke the silence, not even the sullen sounds of sleep. A small light burned in the kitchen.

'Come,' Mrs Hernandez said. 'In the parlour.'

They followed her, and she turned on a floor lamp in the small living-room. The apartment was very clean, but the ceiling plaster was cracked and ready to fall, and the radiator had leaked a big puddle on to the scrubbed linoleum of the floor. The detectives sat facing Mrs Hernandez.

'About your son ...' Carella said at last.

'*Sí*,' Mrs Hernandez said. 'Aníbal would not kill himself.'

'Mrs Hernandez ...'

'No matter what they say, he would not kill himself. This I am sure ... of this. Not Aníbal. My son would not take his own life.'

'Why do you say that, Mrs Hernandez?'

18

'I know. I know.'

'But why?'

'Because I know my son. He is too happy a boy. Always. Even in Puerto Rico. Always happy. Happy people do not kill themselves.'

'How long have you been in the city, Mrs Hernandez?'

'Me, I have been here four years. My husband came first, and then he send for me and my daughter – when it was all right, you know? When he has a job. I leave Aníbal with my mother in Cataño. Do you know Cataño?'

'No,' Carella said.

'It is outside San Juan, across the water. You can see all the city from Cataño. Even La Perla. We live in La Perla before we go to Cataño.'

'What's La Perla?'

'A *fanguito*. How do you say – a slom.'

'A slum?'

'*Sí, sí*, a slum.' Mrs Hernandez paused. 'Even there, even playing in the mud, even hungry sometimes, my son was happy. You can tell a happy person, *señor*. You can tell. When we go to Cataño, it is better, but not so good as here. My husband send for me and Maria. My daughter. She is twenty-one. We come four years ago. Then we send for Aníbal.'

'When?'

'Six months ago.' Mrs Hernandez closed her eyes. 'We pick him up at Idlewild. He was carry his guitar with him. He plays very good the guitar.'

'Did you know your son was a drug addict?' Carella asked.

Mrs Hernandez did not answer for a long time. Then she said, 'Yes,' and she clenched her hands in her lap.

'How long has he been using narcotics?' Kling asked, looking hesitantly at Carella first.

'A long time.'

'How long?'

'I think four months.'

'And he's only been here six months?' Carella asked. 'Did he start in Puerto Rico?'

'No, no, no,' Mrs Hernandez said, shaking her head. '*Señor*, there is very little of this on the island. The narcotics people,

19

they need money, is that not right? Puerto Rico is poor. No, my son learned his habit here, in this city.'

'Do you have any idea how he started?'

'*Sí,*' Mrs Hernandez said. She sighed, and the sigh was a forlorn surrender to a problem too complex for her. She had been born and raised on a sunny island, and her father had cut sugar cane and fished in the off seasons, and there were times when she had gone barefoot and hungry, but there was always the sun and the lush tropical growth. When she got married, her husband had taken her to San Juan, away from the inland town of Comerío. San Juan had been her first city of any size, and she had been caught up in the accelerated pace. The sun still shone, but she was no longer the barefoot adolescent who walked into the village general store and exchanged banter with Miguel, the proprietor. Her first child, Maria, was born when Mrs Hernandez was eighteen. Unfortunately, her husband had lost his job at about the same time, and they moved into La Perla, a historic slum squatting at the foot of Morro Castle. La Perla – The Pearl. Named in high good humour by the poverty-stricken dwellers, for you could strip these people of their belongings, strip them of their clothes, toss them naked into wooden shacks that crouched shoulder to haunches in the mud below the proud walls of the old Spanish fort – but you could not steal their sense of humour.

La Perla, and a girl-child named Maria and two miscarriages that followed in as many years, and then another girl-child who was named Juanita, and then the move to Cataño when Mrs Hernandez's husband found a job there in a small dress factory.

When she was pregnant with Aníbal, the family had gone one Sunday to *El Yunque*, and the *Bosque Nacional del Caribe* – the Rain Forest. And there Juanita, barely two, had crawled to the edge of a fifty-foot precipice while her father was snapping a picture of Mrs Hernandez and his older daughter. The child had made no sound, had screamed not at all, but the plunge had killed her instantly and they came home from the national forest that day with a corpse.

She feared she would lose the baby within her, too. She did not. Aníbal was born, and a christening followed on the heels of a funeral, and then the factory in Cataño closed down and

Mr Hernandez lost his job and took his family back to La Perla again, where Aníbal spent the early years of his boyhood. His mother was twenty-three years old. The sun still shone, but something other than the sun had deepened what used to be laugh wrinkles at the corners of her eyes. Mrs Hernandez was coming to grips with Life. Life and Fortune combined to find more work for Mr Hernandez. Back to Cataño went the family, moving their scant belongings, convinced that this time the move was for good.

It seemed a permanent job. It lasted for many years. Times were good, and Mrs Hernandez laughed a lot, and her husband told her she was still the prettiest woman he knew, and she accepted his lovemaking with hot-blooded passion, and the children – Aníbal and Maria – grew.

When he lost the job that had seemed permanent, Mrs Hernandez suggested leaving the island and heading for the mainland – heading for the city. They had enough for a plane ticket. She packed him a chicken lunch to eat on the plane, and he wore an old Army coat because he had heard the city was very cold, not like Puerto Rico at all, not with the sun shining all the time.

In time, he found a job working on the docks. He sent for Mrs Hernandez and one child, and she took the girl Maria because a girl should not be left without her mother. Aníbal she left with his grandmother. Three and a half years later, he was to be reunited with his family.

Four years later, he was to be an apparent suicide in the basement of a city tenement.

And thinking over the years, the tears started silently on Mrs Hernandez's face, and she sighed again, a sigh as barren and hollow as an empty tomb, and the detectives sat and watched her, and Kling wanted nothing more than to get out of this apartment and its echoes of death.

'Maria,' she said, sobbing. 'Maria started him.'

'Your daughter?' Kling asked incredulously.

'My daughter, yes, my daughter. Both my children. Drug addicts. They . . .' She stopped, the tears flowing freely, unable to speak. The detectives waited.

'I don't know how,' she said at last. 'My husband is good.

He has worked all his life. This minute, this very minute, he is working. And have I not been good? Have I done wrong with my children? I taught them the church, and I taught them God, and I taught them respect for their parents.' Proudly, she said, 'My children spoke English better than anybody in the *barrio*. Americans I wanted them to be. Americans.' She shook her head. 'The city has given us much. Work for my husband, and a home away from the mud. But the city gives with one hand and takes back with the other. And for all, *señores*, for the clean white bathtub in the bathroom, and for the television set in the parlour, I would not trade the sight of my happy children playing in the shadow of the fort. Happy. Happy.'

She bit her lip. She bit it hard. Carella waited for it to bleed, amazed when it did not.

When she released her lip, she sat up straighter in her chair.

'The city,' she said slowly, 'has taken us in. As equals? No, not quite as equals – but this too I can understand. We are new, we are strange. It is always so with the new people, is it not? It does not matter if they are good; they are evil because they are new. But this you can forgive. You can forgive this because there are friends here and relatives, and on Saturday nights it is like being back on the island, with the guitar playing and the laughter. And on Sunday, you go to church, and you say hello in the streets to your neighbours, and you feel good, *señores*, you feel very good, and you can forgive almost everything. You are grateful. You are grateful for almost all of it.

'You can never be grateful for what the city has done to your children. You can never be grateful for the narcotics. You can remember, remember, remember your daughter with young breasts and clean legs and happy eyes until those ... those *bastardos*, those *chulos* ... took her from me. And now my son. Dead. Dead, dead, dead.'

'Mrs Hernandez,' Carella said, wanting to reach out and touch her hand, 'we ...'

'Will it matter that we are Puerto Rican?' she asked suddenly. 'Will you find who killed him anyway?'

'If someone killed him, we'll find him,' Carella promised.

'*Muchas gracias*,' Mrs Hernandez said. 'Thank you. I ... I

know what you must think. My children using drugs, my daughter a prostitute. But, believe me, we . . .'

'Your daughter . . . ?'

'*Sí, sí*, to feed her habit.' Her face suddenly crumpled. It had been fine a moment before, and then it suddenly crumpled, and she sucked in a deep breath, holding back the racking sob, and then she let it out, a sob ripped from her soul. The sob stabbed at Carella, and he could feel himself flinching, could feel his own face tightening in impotency. Mrs Hernandez seemed to be clinging to the edge of a steep cliff. She hung on desperately, and then sighed and looked again to the detectives.

'*Perdóneme*,' she whispered. 'Pardon me.'

'Could we talk to your daughter?' Carella asked.

'*Por favor*. Please. She may help you. You will find her at El Centro. Do you know the place?'

'Yes,' Carella said.

'You will find her there. She . . . she may help you. If she will talk to you.'

'We'll try,' Carella said. He rose. Kling rose simultaneously.

'Thank you very much, Mrs Hernandez,' Kling said.

'*De nada*,' she answered. She turned her head toward the windows. 'Look,' she said. 'It is almost morning. The sun is coming.'

They left the apartment. Both men were silent on the way down to the street.

Carella had the feeling that the sun would never again shine on the mother of Aníbal Hernandez.

CHAPTER FOUR

THE 87th Precinct was bounded on the north by the River Harb and the highway that followed its winding course. Striking south from there, and working block by block across the face of Isola, you first hit Silvermine Road and the fancy apartment buildings facing on the river and Silvermine Park. If you

23

continued walking south, you crossed The Stem, and then Ainsley Avenue, and then Culver Avenue, and the short stretch of Mason known to the Puerto Ricans as 'La Vía de Putas'.

El Centro, despite the occupation of Maria Hernandez, was not located on Whore Street. It crouched in a side-street, one of the thirty-five running blocks that formed the east-to-west territory of the 87th. And though there were Italians and Jews and a large population of Irish people in the 87th, El Centro was in a street that was entirely Puerto Rican.

There were places in the city where you could get anything from a hunk of cocaine to a hunk of woman – anything in the alphabet, from C to S. El Centro was one of them.

The man who owned El Centro lived across the river in the next state. He very rarely visited his establishment. He left it in the capable managerial hands of Terry Donohue, a big Irishman with big fists. Donohue was, for a precinct Irishman, most unusual: he liked Puerto Ricans. This is not to say that he liked only Puerto Rican women. That was certainly true. But there were many 'Americans' in the 87th Precinct who detested the influx of the 'foreigners' while secretly admiring the tight wiggle of a foreign female's backside. Terry liked them both, male and female. He also liked running El Centro. He had worked in dives all over the world, and he was fond of saying El Centro was the worst, but he still liked it.

In fact, Terry Donohue liked just about everything. And, considering the joint he ran, it was surprising that he could find anything to like in a cop – but he liked Steve Carella, and he greeted him warmly when the detective showed up later that day.

'You lop-eared wop!' he shouted. 'I hear you got married!'

'I did,' Carella said, grinning foolishly.

'The poor girl must be nuts,' Terry said, shaking his massive head. 'I'll send her a basket of condolences.'

'The poor girl is in her right mind,' Carella replied. 'She picked the best available man in the city.'

'Hoo! Listen to him!' Terry shouted. 'What's her name, lad?'

'Teddy.'

'Terry?' Terry asked unbelievingly. 'Terry, is it?'

'Teddy. For Theodora.'

24

'And Theodora *what*, may it be?'

'Franklin, it used to be.'

Terry cocked his head to one side. 'An Irish lass, perhaps?'

'Catch me marrying an Irish girl,' Carella said, grinning.

'A mountain guinea like you could do worse than a sweet Irish lass,' Terry said.

'She's Scotch,' Carella told him.

'Good, good!' Terry bellowed. 'I'm four-fifths Irish myself, with a fifth of Scotch thrown in.'

'Ouch!' Carella said.

Terry scratched his head. 'I usually get a laugh from the cops on that one. What're you drinking, Steve?'

'Nothing. I'm here on business.'

'And business was never harmed, by God, by a tiny bit of alcohol.'

'Have you seen Maria Hernandez around?'

'Now, Stevie,' Terry said, 'with a sweet little Scotch lass at home, why would you . . .'

'Business,' Carella said.

'Good,' Terry said. 'A constant man in a city of inconsistencies.'

'Inconstancies,' Carella corrected.

'Whatever, she hasn't been in yet today. Is this about her brother?'

'Yes.'

'A junkie, too, huh?'

'Yes.'

'One thing gets me sore,' Terry said, 'is narcotics. Have you ever seen a pusher in here, Steve?'

'No,' Carella said. 'But I've seen plenty outside on the sidewalk.'

'Sure, because the customer's always right, and he gets what he wants. But you never saw one of those scurvy bastards in my shop, and you never will, that's the truth.'

'When do you expect her?'

'She doesn't roll around until about two. That's if she gets here at all. You know junkies, Steve. Figuring, figuring, always figuring. I swear to God, the president of General Motors doesn't have to do as much conniving as a junkie does.'

Carella glanced at his watch. It was 12.27.

'I'll be back later,' he said. 'I want to grab lunch.'

'You're offending me,' Terry said.

'Huh?'

'Can't you read the sign outside? Bar and *Grill*. Do you see that hot table back there? The best damn lunch in the city.'

'Yeah?'

'*Arroz con pollo* today. Speciality of the house. Got this beautiful little girl who cooks it up.' Terry grinned. 'She cooks by day and hooks by night – but the *arroz con pollo* is out of this world, lad.'

'How's the girl?'

Terry grinned more widely. 'I couldn't say, having only sampled the dear thing's cooking.'

'I've been poisoned in worse places,' Carella said. 'Let's have it.'

Maria Hernandez did not walk into El Centro until three that afternoon. A john from downtown on a romance-seeking excursion would probably have passed her by as a sweet, innocent high-school senior. For whereas the common stereotype puts all prostitutes in tight silk dresses slit to the navel, such is not the case. As a general rule, most of the prostitutes in the 87th were better and more stylishly dressed than the honest women in the streets. They were well-groomed and very often polite and courteous, so much so that many of the little girls in the neighbourhood looked up to the hookers as the cream of society. In much the same way as the pamphlets that go through the mails in a plain brown wrapper, you couldn't tell what these girls had under their covers unless you knew them.

Carella did not know Maria Hernandez. He looked up from his drink when she walked into the bar, and he saw a somewhat slight girl who looked no more than eighteen. Her hair was black, and her eyes were very brown, and she wore a green coat open over a white sweater and a straight black skirt. Like a suburban housewife, she wore nylons and loafers.

'There she is,' Terry said, and Carella nodded.

Maria sat on a stool at the far end of the bar. She nodded hello to Terry, glanced at Carella quickly to ascertain whether or not he was a prospective client, and then fell to staring through the plate glass window at the street. Carella walked over to her.

'Miss Hernandez?' he said.

She swung the stool around. 'Yes?' she said coyly. 'I'm Maria.'

'I'm a cop,' Carella said, figuring he'd set her straight from go, before she wasted any effort.

'I don't know anything about why my brother killed himself,' Maria said, all coyness gone now. 'Any other questions?'

'A few. Shall we sit in a booth?'

'I like it here,' Maria said.

'I don't. A booth or the station house. Take your choice.'

'You get down to business, don't you?'

'I try.'

Maria climbed off the stool. They walked together to a booth opposite the steam table. Maria took off her coat and then slid into the booth opposite Carella.

'I'm listening,' she said.

'How long have you been on the junk?'

'What's that got to do with my brother?'

'How long?'

'About three years.'

'Why'd you start him on it?'

'He asked to start.'

'I don't believe you.'

'Why should I lie to you? He came in the bathroom one night while I was shooting up. The little snot didn't even knock. He wanted to know what I was doing. I gave him a snort.'

'And then?'

'He liked it. He wanted more. You know.'

'I don't know. Tell me about it.'

'He got on mainline a couple of weeks later. End of story.'

'When did you start hustling?'

'Aw, listen . . .' Maria said.

'I can find out.'

'A little while after I got a habit. I had to make money some way, didn't I?'

'I suppose so. Who supplies you?'

'Oh, come on, cop, you know better than that.'

'Who supplied your brother?'

Maria was silent.

'Your brother is dead, do you know that?' Carella said harshly.

'I know it,' Maria answered. 'What do you want me to do? He always was a stupid little snotnose. If he wants to kill himself . . .'

'Maybe he didn't kill himself.'

Maria blinked, seemingly surprised. 'No?' she said cautiously.

'No. Now who supplied him?'

'What difference does it make?'

'Maybe a lot.'

'I don't know anyway.' She paused. 'Listen,' she said, 'why don't you leave me alone? I know cops.'

'Do you?'

'Yeah. You looking for something free, is that it? You figure on scaring me so I'll . . .'

'I'm not looking for anything but information about your brother,' Carella said.

'Yeah, I'll bet.'

'You'd win,' Carella said.

Maria kept staring at him, frowning. 'I know cops who . . .' she started.

'I know hookers with syphilis,' Carella said flatly.

'Listen, you got no right to . . .'

'Then let's drop this whole goddamn routine,' he snapped. 'I want information, period.'

'Okay,' Maria said.

'Okay,' Carella repeated.

'And I still don't know anything,' Maria added.

'You said you started him.'

'Sure.'

'All right, then you probably made a contact for him after he was hooked. Now, who?'

'I didn't make any contact for him. He always went his own way.'

'Maria . . .'

'What do you want from me?' she said, suddenly flaring. 'I don't know anything about my brother. I even found out he was dead from a stranger. I haven't been inside my own house for a year, so how would I know who supplied him or who didn't supply him, or even if he was supplying himself and others besides?'

'Was he pushing?'

'I don't know nothing. I didn't know him any more, can you understand that? If I saw him on the street, I wouldn't recognize him. That's how much I knew about my own brother.'

'You're lying,' Carella said.

'Why should I lie? Who's there to protect? He hung himself, so . . .'

'I told you once,' Carella said. 'Maybe he didn't hang himself.'

'You're making a federal case out of a lousy junkie,' Maria said. 'Why knock yourself out?' Her eyes clouded momentarily. 'He's better off dead, believe me.'

'Is he?' Carella asked. The table was very silent. 'You're holding something back, Maria. What is it?'

'Nothing.'

'What do you know? What is it?'

'Nothing.'

Their eyes met. Carella studied her eyes, and he knew what was in them, and he knew she would tell him nothing more. He had just stared into a pair of opaque hoods. Her eyes had closed her mouth.

'All right,' he said.

The coroner didn't like to deal with new people. That was the way he'd been raised. He hated new faces, and he didn't like to confide secrets to strangers. The coroner's secret was a big one, and Bert Kling was a stranger, and so the coroner studied his face and reluctantly dredged through the facts in his mind, wondering how much he should reveal.

'How come they sent you?' he asked. 'Couldn't they wait for our official report? What's the big rush?'

'Carella asked me to check with you, Dr Soames,' Kling

said. 'I don't know why, but I suppose he wants to get moving on this thing, and he figured he didn't want to wait for the report.'

'Well, I don't know why he couldn't wait for the report,' Soames said. 'Everybody else waits for the report. In all my years here, everybody's waited for the report. So why can't Carella wait?'

'I'd appreciate it if . . .'

'You people think you can just barge in and expect immediate results. You think we have nothing else to do? You know how many corpses we have in there waiting for examination?'

'How many?' Kling asked.

'Don't get factual with me,' Soames advised. 'I'm trying to tell you this is an imposition. If I weren't a gentleman and a doctor, I'd tell you this is a big pain in the ass.'

'Well, I'm sorry to trouble you, really. But . . .'

'If you were really sorry, you wouldn't trouble me. Listen, don't you think I'd love to forget typing up the report? I type with two fingers, and no one on my staff can do any better. Do you know how understaffed I am here? Do you think I can afford to give each case the special attention you're asking for? We've got to process these things like an assembly line. Any break in the routine, and the whole shop goes to pieces. So why don't you wait for the report?'

'Because . . .'

'All right, all right, all right,' Soames said testily. 'All this fuss over a drug addict.' He shook his head. 'Does Carella think this was a suicide?'

'He's . . . I think he's waiting to hear from you people on it. That's why he . . .'

'Do you mean to tell me there's a doubt in his mind?'

'Well, from . . . from outward appearances . . . that is, he's not sure the boy was . . . was asphyxiated.'

'And what do you think, Mr Kling?'

'Me?'

'Yes.' Soames smiled tightly. 'You.'

'I . . . I don't know what to think. This is the first time I . . . I ever saw anybody hanging.'

'Are you familiar with strangulation?'

30

'No, sir,' Kling said.

'Am I supposed to give you a course in medicine? Am I supposed to run a seminar for every uninvited, uninformed detective on the force?'

'No, sir,' Kling said. 'I didn't want . . .'

'We're not talking about a technical hanging now,' Soames said. 'We're not talking about hanging with a hangman's noose, where the bulky knot and the sudden drop break the neck. We're talking about death by strangulation, death by asphyxia. Do you know anything at all about asphyxia, Mr Kling?'

'No, sir. Choking is something I . . .'

'We are not talking about choking, Mr Kling,' Soames said, gaining momentum, annoyed by strangers, equally annoyed by ignorance. 'Choking, in police work, presupposes hands. It is impossible to choke yourself to death. We are now discussing asphyxia induced by pressure on the neck arteries and veins through the use of ropes, wires, towels, handkerchiefs, suspenders, belts, garters, bandages, stockings, or what have you. In the case of Aníbal Hernandez, I understand the alleged means of strangulation was a rope.'

'Yes,' Kling said. 'Yes, a rope.'

'If this were a case of strangulation, pressure from the rope on the neck arteries . . .' Soames paused. 'The neck arteries, Mr Kling, carry blood to the brain. When they are pressed upon, the blood supply is terminated, resulting in anaemia of the brain and loss of consciousness.'

'I see,' Kling said.

'Do you indeed? The pressure on the brain is increased and further aggravated because the veins in the neck are also under pressure from the rope, and there is interference of the return flow of blood through those veins. Eventually, strangulation proper – or asphyxia – will set in and cause the death of the unconscious person.'

'Yes,' Kling said, swallowing.

'Asphyxia, Mr Kling, is defined as the extreme condition caused by lack of oxygen and excess of carbon dioxide in the blood.'

'This is . . . is very interesting,' Kling said weakly.

'Yes, I'm sure it is. The knowledge cost my parents something like twenty thousand dollars. Your own medical education is coming at a much cheaper rate. It's only costing you time, and *my* time at that.'

'Well, I'm sorry if I ...'

'Cyanosis in asphyxia is not uncommon. However ...'

'Cyanosis?'

'The blue coloration. However, as I was about to say, there are other examinations to be made in determining whether or not death was due to asphyxiation. The mucous membranes, for example, and the throat. ... Let it suffice to say, there are many tests. And, of course, cyanosis is present in many types of poisoning.'

'Oh?'

'Yes. We have, considering this poisoning possibility, conducted tests on the urine, the stomach contents, the intestinal contents, the blood, the brain, the liver, the kidneys, the bones, the lungs, the hair and nails, and the muscle tissue.' Soames paused. Dryly, he added, 'We *do* occasionally work here, you know.'

'Yes, I ...'

'Our concern, despite popular misconception, is not chiefly with necrophilism.'

'No, I didn't think it was,' Kling said, not at all sure what the word meant.

'So?' Soames demanded. 'Add it all up, and what do you get? Do you get asphyxia?'

'Do you?' Kling asked.

'You should wait for the report,' Soames said. 'You should really wait for the report. I like to discourage these special requests.'

'Is it asphyxia?'

'No. It is not asphyxia.'

'What then?'

'Alkaloidal poisoning.'

'What's alka—?'

'An overdose of heroin, to be exact. A large overdose. A dose far in excess of the fatal 0·2 gramme.' Soames paused. 'In fact, our young friend Hernandez took enough heroin to kill, if you'll pardon the expression, Mr Kling, a bull.'

CHAPTER FIVE

THERE were about eight million things to do.

There always seemed to be more things wanting doing than a man could possibly get to, and sometimes Peter Byrnes wished for two heads and twice that many arms. With coldly rational illogic, he knew the situation was undoubtedly the same in any kind of business, while simultaneously telling himself that no business could be the rat race police work was.

Peter Byrnes was a detective and a lieutenant, and he headed the squad of bulls who called the 87th Precinct their home. It was, in a somewhat wry way, their home – the way a rusty L.C.I. in the Philippines eventually becomes home to a sailor from Detroit.

The precinct house, in all honesty, was not a very homey place. It did not boast chintz curtains or pop-up toasters or garbage-disposal units or comfortable easy chairs or a dog named Rover who eagerly bounced into the living-room with pipe and slippers. It presented a cold stone façade to Grover Park, which hemmed in the precinct territory on the south. Beyond the façade, just inside the entranceway arch, was a square room with a bare wooden floor and a desk that looked like the judge's bench in a courtroom. A sign on the desk sternly announced: ALL VISITORS MUST STOP AT DESK. When a visitor so stopped, he met either the desk lieutenant or the desk sergeant, both of whom were polite, enthusiastic, and pained in the neck to please the public.

There were detention cells on the ground floor of the building, and upstairs behind mesh-covered windows – mesh-covered because the neighbourhood kids had a delightful penchant for hurling stones at anything faintly smacking of the Law – were the Locker Room, the Clerical office, the Detective Squad Room, and other sundry and comfortable little cubicles, among which were the Men's Room and Lieutenant Byrnes's office.

In defence of the lieutenant's office, it is fair to say there were no urinals lining the walls.

It is also fair to say that the lieutenant liked this office. He had occupied it for a good many years now, and had come to respect it the way a man comes to respect a somewhat threadbare glove he uses for gardening. At times, of course, and especially in a precinct like the 87th, the weeds in the garden grew a little thick. It was at such times that Byrnes devoutly wished for the extra head and arms.

Thanksgiving had not helped at all, and the approaching holidays were making things even worse. It seemed that whenever the holidays rolled around, the people in Byrnes's precinct declared a field day for crime. Knifings in Grover Park, for example, were a year-round occurrence and certainly nothing to get excited about. But with the approach of the holidays, the precinct people burst with Christmas spirit and happily set about the task of decorating the park's scant green patches with rivers of red in honour of the festive season. There had been sixteen knifings in the park during the past week.

The fencing of stolen goods along Culver Avenue was a well-known pastime of the precinct people, too. You could buy anything from a used African witch doctor's mask to a new eggbeater if you happened to come along at the right time with the right amount of cash. This despite the law that made receiving stolen goods a misdemeanour (if the value of such goods was less than $100) and a felony (if the value was more than a C-note). The law didn't disturb the professional shoplifters who toiled by day and sold by night. Nor did it bother the drug addicts who stole to sell to buy to feed their habits. It didn't bother the people who bought the stolen goods, either. Culver Avenue was, in their eyes, the biggest discount house in the city.

It bothered only the cops.

And it bothered them especially during the holiday season. The department stores were very crowded during that joyous season and shoplifters enjoyed the freedom and protective colouring of the sardine pack. And, too, customers for the hot stuff were abundant since there were Christmas lists to worry about, and there was nothing like a fast turnover to spur on a

34

thief to bigger and better endeavours. Everyone, it seemed, was anxious to get his Christmas shopping done early this year, and so Byrnes and his bulls had their hands full.

The prostitutes on Whore Street also had their hands full. Whatever there was about the Yule season that led a man uptown to seek a slice of exotica, Byrnes would never know. But uptown they sought, and Whore Street was the happy hunting ground – and the climactic culmination of a night's sporting was very often a mugging and rolling in an alleyway.

The drinking, too, was beginning to get a little wilder. *What the hell, man has to wet his whistle for the holidays, don't he?* Sure he does, no law against that. But drinking often led to flaring tempers, and flaring tempers often led to the naked revelation of somewhat primitive emotions.

What the hell, man has to slit another man's whistle for the holidays, don't he?

Sure he does.

But when the wetting of a whistle led to the slitting of a whistle, it very often led to the blowing of a whistle by a cop.

All those whistles blowing gave Byrnes a headache. It wasn't that he didn't appreciate music; he simply found the whistle a particularly uninventive instrument.

So Byrnes, though devoutly religious, was devoutly thankful that Christmas came but once a year. It only brought an influx of punks into the Squad Room, and God knew there were enough punks pouring in all year round. Byrnes did not like punks.

He considered dishonesty a personal insult. He had worked for a living since the time he was twelve, and anyone who decided that working was a stupid way to earn money was in effect calling Byrnes a jackass. Byrnes liked to work. Even when it piled up, even when it gave him a headache, even when it included a suicide or homicide or whatever by a drug addict in his precinct, Byrnes liked it.

When the telephone on his desk rang, he resented the intrusion. He lifted the receiver and said, 'Byrnes here.'

The sergeant manning the switchboard behind the desk downstairs said, 'Your wife, Lieutenant.'

'Put her on,' Byrnes said gruffly.

He waited. In a moment, Harriet's voice came on to the line.
'Peter?'

'Yes, Harriet,' he said, and he wondered why women invariably called him Peter, while men called him Pete.

'Are you very busy?'

'I'm kind of jammed, honey,' he said, 'but I've got a moment. What is it?'

'The roast,' she said.

'What about the roast?'

'Didn't I order an eight-pound roast?'

'I guess so. Why?'

'Did I or didn't I, Peter? You remember when we were talking about it and figuring how much we would need? We decided on eight pounds, didn't we?'

'Yes, I think so. What's the matter?'

'The butcher sent five.'

'So send it back.'

'I can't. I called him already and he said he's too busy.'

'Too busy?' Byrnes asked incredulously. 'The butcher?'

'Yes.'

'Well, what the hell else does he have to do but cut meat? I don't under –'

'He'd probably exchange it if I took it down personally. What he meant was that he couldn't spare a delivery boy right now.'

'So take it down personally, Harriet. What's the problem?'

'I can't leave the house, Peter. I'm expecting the groceries.'

'Send Larry down,' Byrnes said patiently.

'He's not home from school yet.'

'I'll be damned if that boy isn't the biggest scholar we ever ...'

'Peter, you know he's re ...'

'... had in the Byrnes family. He's always at school, always ...'

'... hearsing for a school play,' Harriet concluded.

'I've got half a mind to call the principal and tell him ...'

'Nonsense,' Harriet said.

'Well, I happen to like my kid home for supper!' Byrnes said angrily.

'Peter,' Harriet said, 'I don't want to get into a long discussion about Larry or his adolescent pleasures, really I don't. I simply want to know what I should do about the roast.'

'Hell, I don't know. Do you want me to send a squad car to the butcher shop?'

'Don't be silly, Peter.'

'Well, what then? The butcher, so far as I can tell, has committed no crime.'

'He's committed a crime of omission,' Harriet said calmly.

Byrnes chuckled in spite of himself. 'You're too damn smart, woman,' he said.

'Yes,' Harriet admitted freely. 'What about the roast?'

'Won't five pounds suffice? It seems to me we could feed the Russian Army with five pounds.'

'Your brother Louis is coming,' Harriet reminded him.

'Oh.' Byrnes conjured up a vision of his mountainous sibling 'Yes, we'll need the eight pounds.' He paused, thinking. 'Why don't you call the grocer and ask him to hold off on delivery for a few hours? Then you can go down to the butcher and raise all sorts of Irish hell. How does that sound?'

'It sounds fine,' Harriet said. 'You're smarter than you look.'

'I won a bronze scholarship medal in high school,' Byrnes said.

'Yes, I know. I still wear it.'

'Are we set on this roast thing, then?'

'Yes, thank you.'

'Not at all,' Byrnes said. 'About Larry . . .'

'I have to rush to the butcher. Will you be home very late?'

'Probably. I'm really swamped, honey.'

'All right. I won't keep you. Good-bye, dear.'

'Good-bye,' Byrnes said, and he hung up. He sometimes wondered about Harriet, who was, by all civilized standards, a most intelligent woman. She could with the skill of an accountant balance a budget or wade through pages and pages of household figures. She had coped with a policeman-husband who was very rarely home, and had managed to raise a son almost singlehanded. And Larry, despite his damned un-

Byrnesian leaning toward dramatics, was certainly a lad to be proud of. Yes, Harriet was capable, level-headed, and good in bed most of the time.

And yet, on the other hand, something like this roast beef thing could throw her into a confused frenzy.

Women. Byrnes would never understand them.

Sighing heavily, he turned back to his work. He was reading through Carella's D.D. report on the dead boy when the knock sounded on his door.

'Come,' Byrnes said.

The door opened. Hal Willis came into the room.

'What is it, Hal?' Byrnes asked.

'Well, this is a weird one,' Willis said. He was a small man, a man who – by comparison with the other precinct bulls – looked like a jockey. He had smiling brown eyes, and a face that always looked interested, and he also had a knowledge of judo that had knocked many a cheap thief on his back.

'Weird how?' Byrnes asked.

'Desk sergeant put this call through. I took it. But the guy won't speak to anyone but you.'

'Who is he?'

'Well, that's it. He wouldn't give his name.'

'Tell him to go to hell,' Byrnes said.

'Lieutenant, he said it's got something to do with the Hernandez case.'

'Oh?'

'Yeah.'

Byrnes thought for a moment. 'All right,' he said at last. 'Have the call switched to my wire.'

CHAPTER SIX

IT was not that Steve Carella had any theories.

It was simply that the situation stank to high heaven.

Aníbal Hernandez had been found dead at two o'clock on the morning of 18 December. That had been a Monday morning, and now it was Wednesday afternoon, two days later – and the situation still stank to high heaven.

The coroner had reported that Hernandez died of an overdose of heroin, which was not an unseemly way for a hophead to meet his end. The syringe lying next to Hernandez's hand had been scrutinized for latent prints, and those prints were now being compared with the prints lifted from Hernandez's dead fingers.

Carella, with dead certainty, was sure the prints would not match. Someone had tied that rope around Hernandez's neck *after* he was dead, and Carella was willing to bet that the same person had used that syringe to administer the fatal dose of heroin.

Which situation brought up a few problems. Which problems combined to lend the entire situation its air of putrefaction.

For assuming that someone wanted Hernandez dead, an assumption that seemed to be well-founded, and further assuming that someone had used an overloaded syringe of heroin as his murder weapon, why then was the murder weapon not removed from the scene of the crime?

Or why then, for that matter, was the body then hoisted by its own petard, more or less, in an attempt to simulate a hanging suicide?

These were the knotty trivialities that disturbed the normal thinking of Detective Steve Carella. He knew, of course, that there could be a thousand and one motives for murder in the tangled world of drug addiction. He knew, too, that someone unfamiliar with the ways of the coroner's office might innocently hope to palm off a poisoning as a hanging. But he further knew that every man and boy in the United States had been raised on the Fingerprint Legend. *Commit a crime? Wipe off the prints, boy*. The prints had not been wiped from the syringe. The prints were there, as big as life, waiting to be lifted and studied. The syringe was there, too, and if someone were trying to palm off a *hanging*, would he leave a syringe around? Could he be so stupid as to believe the cops wouldn't automatically connect the syringe to a possible death by overdose?

Something stank.

Everything stank.

Carella had a sensitive nose and perhaps a sensitive mind. He walked the streets of the precinct, and he thought, and he wondered where he should begin because the right beginning was very often the most important time-saving device in detective work. And whereas he was, at the moment, primarily concerned with the Hernandez case, he couldn't very well forget the fact that he was a cop being paid to enforce law twenty-four hours a day, three hundred and sixty-five days a year.

When he saw the automobile parked at the kerb near Grover Park, he gave it but a cursory glance. Were he an ordinary citizen out for a mid-afternoon promenade, the cursory glance would have sufficed. Because he was a law-enforcing cop, he took a second glance.

The second glance told him that the car was a 1939 Plymouth sedan, grey, licence number 42L-1731. It told him that the right rear bumper had been smashed in, and it told him that there were two occupants on the back seat, both male, both young. Two young men sitting in the back seat of a car presupposed the absence of a driver. Why were these kids waiting in a car alongside Grover Park, and for whom?

In that instant, Aníbal Hernandez left Carella's mind completely. Casually, he sauntered past the car. The occupants were no more than twenty-one years old. They watched Carella as he passed. They watched him very closely. Carella did not turn to look at the parked car again. He continued walking up the street, and then stepped into the tailor shop of Max Cohen.

Max was a round-faced man with a fringe of white hair that clung to his balding pate like a halo. He looked up when Carella came in, and said, 'Hallo, Stevie, what's new?'

'What could be new?' Carella asked. He had already begun taking off his brown overcoat. Max eyed him curiously.

'Some tellor work, maybe? You want someting sewed?' he asked.

'No. I want to borrow a coat. How about that tan one on the rack? Will it fit me?'

'You vant to borrow . . .?'

'I'm in a hurry, Max. I'll bring it right back. I'm watching some people.'

There was urgency in Carella's voice. Max dropped his

needle and went to the rack of clothing. 'Dun't get it doity, please,' he said. 'It's already been pressed.'

'I won't,' Carella promised. He took the coat from Max, shrugged into it, and then went outside again. The car was still up the street, standing at the kerb alongside the park. The boys were still on the back seat. Carella took a position across the street from the car, standing so that the blind spot in the rear of the car hid him from view. Patiently, he watched.

The third boy appeared some five minutes later. He walked out of the park at a brisk clip, heading directly for the car. Carella shoved himself off the lamp-post instantly and began crossing the street. The third boy did not see him; he walked directly to the car, opened the door on the driver's side, and climbed in. An instant later, Carella threw open the door opposite him.

'Hey, what . . . ?' the driver said.

Carella leaned into the car. His coat was open, and his gun butt lay a few inches from his right hand. 'Sit tight,' he said.

The boys in the back seat exchanged quick, frightened glances.

'Listen, you got no right to . . .' the driver started.

'Shut up,' Carella said. 'What were you doing in the park?'

'Huh?'

'The park. Who'd you meet there?'

'Me? Nobody. I was walking.'

'Where'd you walk?'

'Around.'

'Why?'

'I felt like walking.'

'How come your pals here didn't go with you?'

'They didn't feel like walking.'

'Why are you answering my questions?' Carella hurled.

'What?'

'Why are you answering me, goddamnit? How do you know I'm a cop?'

'. . . I figured . . .'

'Were you expecting cop trouble?'

'Me? No, I was just going for a wa—'

'Empty your pockets!'

'What for?'

'Because I say so!' Carella shouted.

'He's got us cold,' one of the boys in the back seat said.

'Shut up!' the driver snapped without turning his head.

'I'm waiting,' Carella said.

The driver fished into his pocket slowly and cautiously. He placed a package of cigarettes on the seat of the car, and then quickly covered it with a comb, a wallet, and a key ring.

'Hold it,' Carella said. Gingerly, he shoved the package of cigarettes to one side with his forefinger. The cigarettes had been resting on, and covering, a small envelope. Carella picked up the envelope, opened it, spilled some white powder on to the palm of his hand, and then tasted it. The boys watched him silently.

'Heroin,' Carella said. 'Where'd you get it?'

The driver didn't answer.

'You make the buy in the park?'

'I found it,' the driver said.

'Come on! Where'd you buy it?'

'I found it, I told you.'

'Mister, you're getting a possessions charge whether you found it or inherited it. You might be helping yourself if you told me who pushed the junk to you.'

'Leave us out of this,' the boys in the back said. 'We ain't got none of the junk on us. Search us, go ahead. Search us.'

'I'm booking the three of you for acting in concert. Now, who pushed it?'

'I found it,' the driver said.

'Okay, smart guy,' Carella agreed, 'you found it. Have you got a licence to drive this car?'

'Sure I do.'

'Then start driving it.'

'Where to?'

'Take a long guess,' Carella answered. He slid on to the seat and slammed the door behind him.

There was nothing Roger Havilland liked better than questioning suspects, especially when he could question them alone. Roger Havilland was probably the biggest bull in the 87th

Precinct, and undoubtedly the meanest son of a bitch in the world. You couldn't really blame Havilland for his attitude about punks in general. Havilland had once tried to break up a street fight and had in turn had his arm broken in four places. Havilland had been a gentle cop up to that time, but a compound fracture that had to be rebroken and reset because it would not heal properly had not helped his disposition at all. He had come out of the hospital with a healed arm, and a somewhat curious philosophy. Never again would Havilland be caught unawares. Havilland would strike first and ask questions later.

So there was nothing he enjoyed more than questioning suspects, especially when he could question them alone and unassisted. Unfortunately, Carella was with him in the interrogation room on that Wednesday afternoon, 20 December.

The boy who'd been caught with the deck of heroin sat in a chair with his head high and his eyes defiant. The two boys who'd been in the back seat of the car were being questioned separately and respectively by Detectives Meyer and Willis outside. The objective of these related questioning sessions was to discover from whom these kids had made their buy. There was no fun in picking up a hophead. He took a fall, and then the city bore the expense of a thirty-day cold turkey ride. The important man was the pusher. Had the detectives of the 87th wanted to pull in a hundred addicts a day, all of whom would be holding one form or another of narcotics, they had only to walk the streets of their precinct. Unauthorized possession of any quantity of narcotics was a violation of the Public Health Law Section and a misdemeanour. The offender would undoubtedly pull a term on Bailey's Island – thirty days or more – and then come out ready to seek the drug again.

On the other hand, the pusher was in a more vulnerable position. State law made the possession of certain quantities of narcotics a felony, and those quantities were:

1. One-quarter ounce or more of one-per-cent compounds of heroin, morphine, or cocaine.
2. Two ounces or more of other narcotics.

And this possession was punishable by imprisonment of from

one to ten years. Then, too, the possession of two or more ounces aggregate weight of compounds containing three per cent or more of heroin, morphine, or cocaine – or sixteen ounces or more of other narcotics – created, according to the law, an unrebuttable presumption of intent to sell.

It was not a crime to be a drug addict, but things could be made tough for you if you possessed either drugs or instruments for using drugs, which possession *was* a crime.

The boy who'd made his buy in Grover Park had been caught holding a sixteenth of H, which had probably cost him something like five bucks. He was small fry. The bulls of the 87th were interested in the man who'd sold the stuff to him.

'What's your name?' Havilland asked the boy.

'Ernest,' the boy answered. He was tall and thin, with a shock of blond hair that hung on to his forehead dejectedly now.

'Ernest what?'

'Ernest Hemingway.'

Havilland looked at Carella and then turned back to the boy. 'All right, champ,' he said, 'we'll try again. What's your name?'

'Ernest Hemingway.'

'*I got no time to waste with a wise punk!*' Havilland shouted.

'What's the matter with you?' the boy said. 'You asked me what my name was, and I –'

'If you don't want to be picking up your teeth in a minute, you'd better give me a straight answer. What's your name?'

'Ernest Hemingway. Listen, what's with –'

Havilland slapped the boy quickly and almost effortlessly. The boy's head rocked to one side, and Havilland drew his hand back for another blow.

'Lay off, Rog,' Carella said. 'That's his name. It's on his draft card.'

'Ernest *Hem*ingway?' Havilland asked incredulously.

'What's the matter with that?' Hemingway asked. 'Listen, what's bugging you guys, anyway?'

'There's a fellow,' Carella said. 'A writer. His name is Ernest Hemingway, too.'

'Yeah?' Hemingway said. He paused, then thoughtfully said, 'I never heard of him. Can I sue him?'

'I doubt it,' Carella said dryly. 'Who sold you that sixteenth?'

44

'Your writer friend,' Hemingway answered, smirking.

'This is going to be cute,' Havilland said. 'I like them when they're cute. Kid, you are going to wish you were never born.'

'Listen, kid,' Carella said, 'you're only making things tough for yourself. You can get thirty out of this or ninety, depending on how cooperative you are. You might even get a suspended sentence, who can tell?'

'You promising?'

'I can't make promises. It's up to the judge. But if he knows you helped us nail a pusher, he might be inclined toward leniency.'

'Do I look like a stoolie?'

'No,' Havilland answered. 'Most stoolies are better looking than you.'

'What was this lug before he turned cop?' Hemingway asked. 'A television comic?'

Havilland smiled and then slapped Hemingway across the mouth.

'Put your hands away,' Carella said.

'I don't have to take crap from a snotnose junkie. I don't have to –'

'Put your goddamn hands away!' Carella said, more loudly this time. 'You feel like a workout, go down to the Headquarters gym.'

'Listen, I –'

'How about it, kid?' Carella asked.

'Who the hell do you think you are, Carella?' Havilland wanted to know.

'Who the hell do you think *you* are, Havilland?' Carella said. 'If you don't want to question this kid properly, then get the hell out. He's my prisoner.'

'You'd think I broke his head or something,' Havilland said petulantly.

'I don't want to give you the opportunity,' Carella said. He turned back to Hemingway. 'How about it, son?'

'Don't give me the "son" routine, cop. I blab who pushed the junk, and I'll still go the limit.'

'Maybe you'd like us to say we found you with a quarter instead of a sixteenth,' Havilland suggested.

'You can't do that, big mouth,' Hemingway said.

'We pulled in enough narcotics today to fill a steamboat,' Havilland lied. 'Who's to know what *you* were carrying?'

'You know it was a sixteenth,' Hemingway said, weakening.

'Sure, but who else besides us knows it? You can get ten years for holding a quarter-ounce, pal. Slap on to that the intent to sell the junk to your pals outside.'

'Who was trying to sell it? Jesus, I only bought it! And it was a sixteenth, not a quarter!'

'Yeah,' Havilland said. 'But it's a pity we're the only ones who know that, ain't it? Now, what's the pusher's name?'

Hemingway was silent, thinking

'Possession of a quarter-ounce with intent to sell,' Havilland said to Carella. 'Let's wrap this up, Steve.'

'Hey, wait a minute,' Hemingway said. 'You're not gonna railroad me like that, are you?'

'Why not?' Havilland said. 'You're no relative of mine.'

'Well, can't we . . .' Hemingway stopped. 'Can't we . . .'

'The pusher,' Carella said.

'A guy named Gonzo.'

'Is that his first name or his last?'

'I don't know.'

'How'd you contact him?'

'This was the first I heard of him,' Hemingway said. 'Today, I mean. The first time I ever copped from him.'

'Yeah, sure,' Havilland said.

'I snow you not,' Hemingway answered. 'I used to buy from another kid. The meet was in the park, near the lion house. I used to get from this other kid there. So today, I go to the meet, and there's this new character. He tells me his name is Gonzo, and he's got good junk. So, okay, I gambled on getting beat stuff. Then the law showed.'

'What about the two kids in the back seat?'

'Skin poppers. You want to be smart, you'll throw them out. This whole business has scared them blue.'

'This is your first fall?' Carella asked.

'Yeah.'

'How long have you been on the junk?'

'About eight years.'

'Mainline?'

Hemingway looked up. 'There's another way?' he asked.

'Gonzo, huh?' Havilland said.

'Yeah. Listen, you think I'll be able to get a fix soon? I mean, I'm beginning to feel a little sick, you dig me?'

'Mister,' Havilland said, 'consider yourself cured.'

'Huh?'

'They don't meet near the lion house where you're going.'

'I thought you said I might get a suspended sentence.'

'You might. Do you expect us to keep you hopped up until then?'

'No, but I thought ... Jesus, ain't there a doctor or something around?'

'Who'd you used to buy from?' Carella asked.

'What do you mean?'

'At the lion house. You said this Gonzo was new. Who pushed to you before?'

'Oh. Yeah, yeah. Listen, can't we talk a doctor into fixing me? You know, I mean, like I'll puke all over the floor or something.'

'We'll give you a mop,' Havilland said.

'Who was the other pusher?' Carella asked again.

Hemingway sighed wearily. 'A kid named Annabelle.'

'A broad?' Havilland asked.

'No, some spic kid. Annabelle. That's a spic name.'

'Aníbal?' Carella asked, his scalp prickling.

'Yeah.'

'Aníbal what?'

'Fernandez, Hernandez, Gomez? Who can tell with these spics? They all sound alike to me.'

'Was it Aníbal Hernandez?'

'Yeah, I think so. Yeah, that sounds as good as any. Listen, can't I get a fix? I mean, I'll puke.'

'Go ahead,' Havilland said. 'Puke.'

Hemingway sighed heavily again, and then he frowned, and then he lifted his head and asked, 'Is there *really* a writer named Ernest Hemingway?'

CHAPTER SEVEN

THE lab report on the rope and the I.B. report on the finger-prints came in later that afternoon. There was only one piece of information in either of them that surprised Carella.

He was not surprised to learn that an analysis of the rope found around Hernandez's neck completely discounted the possibility of the boy having hanged himself. A rope, you see, has peculiar properties of its own, among which are the fibres of which it is constructed. Had Hernandez hanged himself, he undoubtedly would have first tied one end of the rope on the barred window, then tied the other end around his neck, and then leaned into the rope, cutting off his oxygen supply.

The fibres on the rope, however, were flattened in such a way as to indicate that the body had been pulled *upwards*. In short, the rope had first been affixed to Hernandez's neck and then the loose end had been threaded through the bars and pulled upon until the body assumed its leaning position. The contact of the rope's fibres with the steel of the bar had given the fibres a telltale direction. Hernandez may have administered his own fatal dose of heroin, but he had certainly not strung himself to the barred window.

The fingerprints found on the syringe seemed to discount the possibility of suicide completely, and this hardly surprised Carella either. None of the fingerprints – and there were a good many, all from the same person, all clear sharp prints – matched up with the fingerprints of Aníbal Hernandez. If he had used the syringe at all, then he had wiped it clean before handing it to a second unknown party.

The *unknown* party bit was the part that surprised Carella. The Identification Bureau had done a runthrough on the prints, and come up with a blank. Whoever had handled the syringe, whoever had allegedly pumped that heroin into Hernandez, did not have a criminal record. Of course, the F.B.I. had not yet been heard from, but Carella was none the less disappointed. In his secret heart, he was halfway hoping that someone who had access to a syringe and the staggering amount of heroin it had taken to kill Hernandez would also be someone with a record.

He was mulling over his disappointment when Lieutenant Byrnes poked his head out of the office.

'Steve,' he called. 'See you a moment?'

'Yes, sir,' Carella said. He rose and walked to Byrnes's door. The lieutenant was silent until Carella closed the door.

'Bad break, huh?' he asked then.

'Sir?'

'Couldn't get a make on those fingerprints.'

'Oh, no. I was kind of hoping we would.'

'I was, too,' Byrnes said.

The two men stared at each other thoughtfully.

'Is there a copy around?'

'Of the prints?'

'Yes.'

'May I have it?'

'Well, it's already been checked. I mean, we couldn't . . .'

'I know, Steve. It's just that I have an idea I want to . . . to work on.'

'About the Hernandez case?'

'More or less.'

'Feel like airing it?'

'No, Steve.' He paused. 'Not yet.'

'Sure,' Carella said. 'Whenever you feel like.'

'Get me those prints before you check out, will you, Steve?' Byrnes asked, smiling weakly.

'Sure,' Carella said. 'Will that be all?'

'Yes, go ahead. You're probably anxious to get home.' He paused. 'How's the wife?'

'Oh, fine,' Carella said.

'Good, good. It's important to have . . .' Byrnes shook his head and let the sentence trail. 'Well, go ahead, Steve, don't let me keep you.'

He was bushed when he got home that night. Teddy greeted him at the door, and he kissed her in a perfunctory, most un-newlywedlike way. She looked at him curiously, led him to a drink waiting in the living-room and then, attuned to his uncommunicative mood, went out to the kitchen to finish dinner. When she served the meal, Carella remained silent.

And because Teddy had been born with neither the capacity for speech nor the capacity for hearing, the silence in the small kitchen was complete. She looked at him often, wondering if she had offended him in some way, longing to see words on his lips, words she could read and understand. And finally, she reached across the table and touched his hand, and her eyes opened wide in entreaty, brown eyes against an oval face.

'No, it's nothing,' Carella said gently.

But still her eyes asked their questions. She cocked her head to one side, the short raven hair sharply detailed against the white wall behind her.

'This case,' he admitted.

She nodded, waiting, relieved that he was troubled with his work and not with his wife.

'Well, why the hell would anyone leave a perfect set of fingerprints on a goddamn murder weapon, and then leave the weapon where every rookie cop in the world could find it?'

Teddy shrugged sympathetically, and then nodded.

'And why try to simulate a hanging afterwards? Does the killer think he's dealing with a pack of nitwits, for Christ's sake?' He shook his head angrily. Teddy shoved back her chair and then came around the table and plunked herself down in his lap. She took his hand and wrapped it around her waist, and then she snuggled up close to him and kissed his neck.

'Stop that,' he told her, and then – realizing she could not see his lips because her face was buried in his throat – he caught her hair and gently yanked back her head, and repeated, 'Stop it. How can I think about the case with you doing that?'

Teddy gave an emphatic nod of her head, telling her husband that he had exactly understood her motivations.

'You're a flesh pot,' Carella said, smiling. 'You'll destroy me. Do you think . . .'

Teddy kissed his mouth.

Carella moved back gently. 'Do you think you'd leave a . . .'

She kissed him again, and this time he lingered a while before moving away.

'. . . syringe with fingerprints all over it on a mmmmmmmm . . .'

Her face was very close to his, and he could see the brightness in her eyes, and the fullness of her mouth when she drew back.

'Oh God, woman,' he said.

She rose and took his hand and as she was leading him from the room he turned her around and said, 'The dishes. We have to . . .' and she tossed up her back skirts in reply, the way can-can dancers do. In the living-room, she handed him a sheet of paper, neatly folded in half.

'I didn't know you wanted to answer the mail,' Carella said. 'I somehow suspected I was being seduced.'

Impatiently, Teddy gestured to the paper in his hand. Carella unfolded it. The white sheet was covered with four typewritten stanzas. The stanzas were titled: ODE FOR STEVE.

'For me?' he asked.

Yes, she nodded.

'Is this what you do all day, instead of slaving around the house?'

She wiggled her forefinger, urging him to read the poem.

ODE FOR STEVE

I love you, Steve,
I love you so.
I want to go
Where e'er you go.

In counterpoint,
And conversely,
When you return
'Twill be with me.

So darling boy,
My message now
Will follow with
A courtly bow:

You go, I go;
Return, return I;
Stay, go, come –
Together.

51

'The last stanza doesn't rhyme,' Carella said.

Teddy pulled a mock mask of stunned disgust.

'Also, methinks I read sexual connotations into this thing,' Carella added.

Teddy waved one hand airily, shrugged innocently, and then – like a burlesque queen imitating a high-priced fashion model – walked gracefully and suggestively into the bedroom, her buttocks wiggling exaggeratedly.

Carella grinned and folded the sheet of paper. He put it into his wallet, walked to the bedroom door, and leaned against the jamb.

'You know,' he said, 'you don't have to write poems.'

Teddy stared at him across the length of the room. He watched her, and he wondered briefly why Byrnes wanted a copy of the fingerprints, and then he said huskily, 'All you have to do is ask.'

All Byrnes wanted to do was ask.

The lie, as he saw it, was a two-part lie, and once he asked about it, it would be cleared up. Which was why he sat in a parked automobile, waiting. In order to ask, you have to find the askee. You find that person, you corner that person, and you say, 'Now listen to me, is it true you . . .?'

Or was that the way?

What was the way, damnit, what was the way, and how had a man who'd lived honestly all his life suddenly become enmeshed in something like this? No! No, damnit, it was a lie. A stupid lie because there was a body and someone was trying to . . . but suppose it were not a lie?

Suppose the first part of the lie was true, just the first part alone, what then? Then, then, then something would have to be done. What? What do I say if the first part of the lie is true? How do I handle it? This first part of the lie, this first thing was enough. It was enough to cause a man to doubt his sanity, if it was true, if this first thing was true, no, no, it cannot be true!

But maybe it is. Face that possibility. Face the possibility that at least the first thing may be true, and plan on handling it from there.

And if this other thing was true, and if it broke, what untold harm would be done then? Not only to Byrnes himself, but to Harriet, God, why should Harriet have to suffer, Harriet so innocent, and the police department, how would it look for the police department, oh Jesus let it not be true, let it be a lousy punk lie.

He sat in the parked car and he waited, certain he would recognize him when he came out of the building. The building was in Calm's Point, where Byrnes lived, and it was surrounded by lawn, and there were trees placed all around it, trees bare now with winter, their roots clutching frozen earth, the bases of their trunks caked with snow. There were lights burning in the building, and the lights were a warm amber against the cold winter sky, and Byrnes watched the lights and wondered.

He was a compact man, Byrnes, with a head like a rivet. His eyes were blue and tiny, but they didn't miss very much, and they were set in a browned and weathered face that was seamed with wrinkles. His nose was craggy like the rest of his face, and his mouth was firm with a weak upper lip and a splendid lower lip. He had a chin like a cleft boulder, and his head sat low on his shoulders, as if it were hunched in defence. He sat in the car, and he watched his own breath plume whitely from his lips, and he reached over to wipe the fogged windshield with a gloved hand, and then he saw the people coming from the building.

Young people, laughing and joking. A boy stopped to roll a snowball and hurl it at a young girl who shrieked in gleeful terror. The boy chased her into the shadows then, and Byrnes watched, searching for a face and figure he could recognize. There were more people now. Too many to watch without being close. Hastily, Byrnes stepped out of the car. The cold attacked his face instantly. He hunched his shoulders and walked toward the building.

'Hello, Mr Byrnes,' a boy said, and Byrnes nodded and studied the faces of the other boys who were swarming past. And then suddenly, as if a dam hole had been plugged, the tide stopped. He turned and watched the kids as they sauntered away, and then he sucked in a deep breath and started up the steps, passing beneath an arch upon which were chiselled the words CALM'S POINT HIGH SCHOOL.

He had not been inside this building once since his visit during Open School Week back in ... how many years had it been? Byrnes shook his head. *A man should take more care*, he thought. A man should watch these things. But how could anyone have even suspected, and how could anyone have prevented, Harriet, Harriet, she should have watched more carefully, if this thing is true, *if* it is true.

The auditorium, he supposed. That was where they'd be. If there were any more of them, they would be in the auditorium. The school was very quiet, closed for the night, and he could hear the hollow tattoo of his own shoes against the marbled main floor of the building. He found the auditorium by instinct, and he smiled wryly, reflecting that he wasn't such a bad detective after all, Christ, what would this thing do to the police department?

He opened the door. A woman stood at the far end of the auditorium, near the piano. Byrnes pulled back his shoulders and started down the long aisle. The woman was the only other person in the large, high-ceilinged room. She looked up expectantly as he approached her. She was in her mid forties, a stoutish woman who wore her hair in a bun at the back of her neck. She had a mild, pleasant face with cowlike brown eyes.

'Yes?' she asked, her head lifted, her eyebrows lifted, her voice lifted. 'May I help you?'

'Perhaps so,' Byrnes said, mustering up a genial smile. 'Is this where you're rehearsing the senior play?'

'Why, yes,' the woman said. 'I'm Miss Kerry. I'm directing the show.'

'How do you do,' Byrnes said. 'I'm very happy to know you.'

He felt suddenly awkward. His mission, he felt, was a basically secretive one, and he did not feel like exchanging pleasant cordialities with a high-school teacher.

'I saw the boys and girls leaving,' he said.

'Yes,' Miss Kerry replied, smiling.

'I thought since I was in the neighbourhood, I'd stop by and give my son a lift home. He's in the show, you know.' Byrnes forced another smile. 'Talks about it at home all the time.'

'Oh, is that right?' Miss Kerry said, pleased.

'Yes. But I didn't see him outside with the other kids. I was wondering if you ...' He glanced up at the darkened empty stage. '... had him in here working with the ...' His sentence lost momentum. '... sets or ... or something.'

'You probably missed him,' Miss Kerry said. 'The cast and crew all left just a few minutes ago.'

'All of them?' Byrnes asked. 'Larry, too?'

'Larry?' Miss Kerry frowned momentarily. 'Oh, yes, Larry. Of course. Yes, I'm sorry, but he left with the others.'

Byrnes felt an enormous sense of relief. If nothing else, the show accounted for his son's evenings. He had not lied on that score. The smile mushroomed on to his face. 'Well,' he said, 'I'm sorry to have troubled you.'

'Not at all. It's I who should apologize, not remembering Larry's name instantly. He's the only Larry working on the show, and he's really doing a fine job.'

'Well, I'm glad to hear that,' Byrnes said.

'Yes, Mr Schwartz,' Miss Kerry replied, 'you should be very proud of your son.'

'Well, I am. I'm happy to hear ...' Byrnes stopped. He stared at Miss Kerry for a long, terrible moment.

'My son is Larry *Byrnes*,' he said.

Miss Kerry frowned. 'Larry Byrnes. Oh, I'm sorry. I mean ... your son isn't in the show at all. Did he say he was? That is ... well, he didn't even try out for it.'

'I see,' Byrnes said tightly.

'I do hope I haven't ... that is, well, perhaps the boy had reasons of his own for wanting you to believe he was ... well ... you can't always take these things on face value, Mr Byrnes. The boy undoubtedly had reasons.'

'Yes,' Byrnes said sadly. 'I'm afraid he had.'

He thanked Miss Kerry again, and then left her in the big, empty auditorium.

CHAPTER EIGHT

BYRNES sat in the living-room and listened to the methodically monotonous tocking of the grandfather clock. The clock had always been a comfort to him, a possession he'd desired ever since he'd been a boy. He could not have told why he'd wanted a grandfather clock for his own, but he had wanted one, and one day he and Harriet had driven out to the country and stopped at an old barn repainted red and white, displaying the sign ANTIQUES.

The proprietor of the shop had been a thin, wispish man with an effeminate walk, dressed like a country squire, complete with waistcoat and leather-elbow-patched sports jacket. He had floated around among his rare pieces of china and cut glass, fluttering anxiously whenever Harriet lifted a piece of crockery. Eventually, they had got around to the grandfather clock. There were several clocks, and one was going for $573, and had been made in England, and was signed and dated by the craftsman who had fashioned it. It was still in fine working order, a stately, proud time-telling machine. Another clock had been made in America, and it was unsigned and undated, and it would probably need repairs – but it cost only $200.

When the proprietor saw that Byrnes's interest was in the cheaper clock, he immediately disqualified them as true *aficionados*. Caustically, he said, 'Well, of course, if you want the *garden* variety of grandfather clock,' and then concluded the deal with barely disguised distaste. Byrnes had taken his garden variety of grandfather clock home. The local jeweller had charged $14 to set it in fine running condition. It had never given Byrnes a bit of trouble since. It stood now in the hallway, and it tocked off the minutes in a deep monotonous voice, and its delicately wrought hands held the white moon face in a wide-angled grin, and the grin read ten minutes to two.

There was no comfort in the clock now, no comfort in the ordered, well-regulated spacing of its breathing. There was neither – and curiously – a sense of time attached to the clock. There was instead a desperate feeling of urgency, the hands advancing, the mechanism whirring, as if time-disconnected, separate and apart from the living universe, the clock would suddenly clasp its own hands and then explode into the hallway leaving Byrnes alone, waiting for his son.

The house creaked.

He had never before noticed how the house creaked. There was sound everywhere around him, the sound of an old man with rheumatic joints. From the bedroom upstairs, he could hear Harriet deep in slumber, the sound of her even breathing superimposed on the dread tocking of the clock and the uneasy groaning of the house.

And then Byrnes heard a small sound that was like an ear-splitting thundercrack, the sound he had been waiting for and listening for all night long, the sound of a key being turned in the front-door latch. All other sounds vanished in that moment. He sat tensed and alert in his chair while the key twisted, and then the door swung wide, creaking a little, and he could hear the malicious gossip of the wind outside, and then the door quietly easing shut and snuggling into the jamb, and then the boards in the hallway creaking as feet fell upon them.

'Larry?' he called.

His voice reached out of the darkened living-room, and fled into the hollows of the house. For a moment, there was complete silence, and then Byrnes was aware of the tocking of the grandfather clock again, his garden-variety clock complacently standing against the wall and watching life rush by, like an idler leaning against the plate-glass window of a corner drug store.

'Dad?' The voice was surprised, and the voice was young, and the voice was a little breathless, the way a voice will sound when its owner has come into a warm room after facing a sullen cold outside.

'In here, Larry,' he said, and again the silence greeted him, a calculating silence this time, broken only by the steady punctuality of the clock.

'Sure,' Larry said, and Byrnes listened to his footfalls as he came through the house and then paused outside the living-room door.

'Okay to put on a light?' Larry asked.

'Yes, go ahead,' Byrnes said.

Larry came into the room, walking with the familiar skill of a person who has occupied a house for a long time, walking in the darkness directly to an end table and then turning on a lamp there.

He was a tall boy, much taller than his father. His hair was red, and his face was long and thin, with his father's craggy nose, and his mother's guileless grey eyes. His chin was weak, Byrnes noticed, nor would it ever be any stronger because adolescence had forged the boy's face, and it was set now for eternity. He wore a sports shirt and slacks, over which had been thrown a sports jacket. Byrnes wondered if he'd left his overcoat in the hallway.

'Doing some reading?' Larry asked. His voice was no longer the voice of a child. It sprang full-chested and deep from the long, reedy body, and somehow it sounded ludicrous in a boy so young, a boy hardly eighteen.

'No,' Byrnes said. 'I was waiting for you.'

'Oh?' Byrnes watched his son, listening to him, amazed at how the single word 'Oh?' could have conveyed so much sudden wariness and caution.

'Where were you, Larry?' Byrnes asked. He watched his son's face, hoping his son would not lie, telling himself a lie would shatter him now, a lie would destroy him.

'At school,' Larry said, and Byrnes took the lie, and it did not hurt as much as he expected it would, and suddenly something inside the man took over, something alien to a father-son relationship, something he reserved for the squad room at the 87th. It came into his head and on to his tongue with the ready rapidity of years of familiarity. In the space of three seconds, Peter Byrnes became a cop questioning a suspect.

'The high school?'

'Yes, Dad.'

'Calm's Point High, isn't it? Isn't that where you go?'

'Don't you know, Dad?'

'I'm asking you.'

58

'Yes. Calm's Point.'

'Late to be getting home, isn't it?'

'Is that what this is all about?' Larry asked.

'What kept you so late?'

'We're rehearsing, you know that.'

'For what?'

'The senior play. Holy cow, Dad, we've only gone over this about a hundred times.'

'Who else is in the play?'

'Lots of kids.'

'Who's directing it?'

'Miss Kerry.'

'What time did you start rehearsals?'

'Hey, what is this?'

'What time did you break up?'

'About one o'clock, I guess. Some of the kids stopped for a soda afterwards.'

'The rehearsal broke up at ten-thirty,' Byrnes said clearly. 'You weren't there. You're not in the play, Larry. You never were. Where did you spend the time between three-thirty yesterday afternoon and two o'clock this morning?'

'Jesus!' Larry said.

'Don't swear in my house,' Byrnes said.

'Well, for Christ's sake, you sound like a district attorney.'

'Where were you, Larry?'

'Okay, I'm not in the play,' Larry said. 'Okay? I didn't want to tell Mom. I got kicked out after the first few rehearsals. I guess I'm not a good actor. I guess ...'

'You're a terrible actor, and a bad listener. You were *never* in the play, Larry. I said that just a few seconds ago.'

'Well ...'

'Why'd you lie? What have you been doing?'

'Now what would I be doing?' Larry said. 'Listen, Dad, I'm sleepy. If you don't mind, I'd like to get to bed.'

He was starting from the room when Byrnes shouted, 'I DO MIND! COME BACK HERE!'

Larry turned slowly to face his father. 'This isn't your grubby squad room, Pop,' he said. 'Don't yell at me like one of your lackeys.'

'This has been my squad room longer than the 87th has,' Byrnes said tightly. 'Wipe the sneer out of your voice, or I'll kick your ass all over the street.'

Larry's mouth fell open. He stared at Byrnes for a moment, and then said, 'Listen, Dad, I'm really ...'

Byrnes came up out of the chair suddenly. He walked to his son and said, 'Empty your pockets.'

'What?'

' I said ...'

'Oh now, let's just hold this a minute,' Larry said heatedly. 'Now, let's just slow down. What the hell is this, anyway? Don't you play cop enough hours a day, you have to come home ...'

'Shut up, Larry, I'm warning you!'

'Shut up yourself! For Christ's sake, I don't have to take this kind of ...'

Byrnes slapped his son suddenly and viciously. He slapped him with an opened, calloused hand that had been working since its owner was twelve years old, and that hand slapped Larry hard enough to knock him off his feet.

'Get up!' Byrnes said.

'You better not hit me again,' Larry muttered.

'*Get up!*' Byrnes reached down, catching his son's collar with his hand. He yanked him to his feet, and then pulled him close and then said through clenched teeth, 'Are you a drug addict?'

Silence crowded into the room, filling every corner.

'Wh ... what?' Larry asked.

'Are you a drug addict?' Byrnes repeated. He was whispering now, and the whisper was loud in the silent room. The clock in the hallway added its voice, commenting in a monotone.

'Who ... who told you?' Larry said at last.

'Are you?'

'I ... I fool around a little.'

'Sit down,' Byrnes said wearily.

'Dad, I ...'

'Sit down,' Byrnes said. 'Please.'

Larry sat in the chair his father had vacated. Byrnes paced

the room for several moments, and then stopped before Larry and asked, 'How bad is it?'

'Not too bad.'

'Heroin?'

'Yes.'

'How long?'

'I've been on for about four months now.'

'Snorting?'

'No. No.'

'Skin pops?'

'Dad, I . . .'

'Larry, Larry, are you mainlining?'

'Yes.'

'How'd you start?'

'At the school. Some kid was shoving muggles. Marijuana, Dad. We call it . . .'

'I know the names,' Byrnes said.

'So that's how I started. Then I forget, I think I had a snort of C, and then somebody gave me a snort of H, and that . . . Well, I tried a skin pop.'

'How long before you went on mainline?'

'About two weeks.'

'Then you're hooked solid,' Byrnes said.

'I can take it or leave it alone,' Larry answered defiantly.

'Sure. Where do you get your stuff?'

'Listen, Dad . . .'

'I'm asking as a father, not a cop!' Byrnes said quickly.

'Up . . . up in Grover Park.'

'From whom?'

'What difference does it make? Look, Pop, I . . . I'll ditch the habit, okay? I mean, really, I will. But let's knock this off. It's kind of embarrassing, you know?'

'It's more embarrassing than you think. Did you know a boy named Aníbal Hernandez?'

Larry was silent.

'Look, son, you went all the way to Isola to buy. You bought in my precinct, in Grover Park. Did you know Aníbal Hernandez?'

'Yes,' Larry admitted.

'How well?'

'I bought from him a coupla times. He was a mule, Dad. That means he pushed to other kids. Mostly because he had a habit himself.'

'I know what a mule is,' Byrnes said patiently. 'How many times, exactly, did you buy from him?'

'A coupla times, I told you.'

'Twice, you mean?'

'Well, more than that.'

'Three times?'

'No.'

'Four? For God's sake, Larry, *how many times*?'

'Well, like ... well, to tell you the truth, I bought from him mostly. I mean, you know, you fall in with a pusher and if he gives you good stuff you stick with him. Anyway, he ... he was a nice guy. Few times we ... we shot up together, you know? Free. I mean, he didn't charge me anything for the junk. He laid it on me free. He was all right.'

'You keep saying *was*. Do you know he's dead?'

'Yes. He hanged himself, I heard.'

'Now listen to me carefully, Larry. I received a phone call the other day. The caller ...'

'From who?'

'An anonymous call. I took it because it was related to the Hernandez death. This was before we got the coroner's report.'

'Yeah?'

'The caller told me a few things about you.'

'Like what? Like I'm a junkie, you mean?'

'Not only that.'

'What then?'

'He told me where you were and what you were doing on the night of December 17th, and the early morning of December 18th.'

'Yeah?'

'Yes.'

'So where was I supposed to have been?'

'In a basement room with Aníbal Hernandez.'

'Yeah?'

'That's what the caller told me.'

'So?'

'Is it true?'

'Maybe.'

'Larry, don't get smart again! So help me God, I'll ...'

'Okay, okay, I was with Annabelle.'

'From what time to what time?'

'From about ... let me see ... it must have been nine o'clock. Yeah, from about nine to midnight, I guess. That's right. I left him about twelve or so.'

'Were you with him at all that afternoon?'

'No. I met him in the street about nine. Then we went down to the basement.'

'When you left him, did you come straight home?'

'No. I was high. Annabelle was already nodding on the cot, and I didn't want to fall asleep there. So I cut out, and I walked around a little.'

'How high were you?'

'High,' Larry said.

'What time did you get home?'

'I don't know. Very late.'

'What's very late?'

'Three, four.'

'Were you alone with Hernandez until midnight?'

'Yes.'

'And he shot up, too, is that right?'

'Yes.'

'And you left him asleep?'

'Well, nodding. You know – not here, not there.'

'How much did Hernandez shoot?'

'We split a sixteenth.'

'Are you sure?'

'Sure, Annabelle said so when he took out the deck. He said it was a sixteenth. I'll tell you the truth, I'm glad we shot up together. I hate to shoot up alone. It scares me. I'm afraid of an overdose.'

'You say you shot up together? Did you both use the same syringe?'

'No. Annabelle had his spike, and I had mine.'

63

'And where's your outfit now?'

'I got it. Why?'

'You still have your syringe?'

'Certainly.'

'Tell me exactly what happened.'

'I don't follow you.'

'After Annabelle showed you the deck.'

'I got out my spike, and he got out his. Then we cooked the stuff in some bottle caps, and . . .'

'The caps found on that orange crate under the light?'

'Yeah, I guess so. Yeah, there was an orange crate across the room.'

'Did you take the syringes with you when you went to that orange crate?'

'No, I don't think so. We left them on the cot, I think.'

'Then what?'

'We cooked the junk and went back to the cot, and Annabelle picked up his spike, and I picked up mine, and we loaded them and fixed ourselves.'

'Annabelle picked up his syringe first?'

'Yes, I think so.'

'Is it possible he picked up the wrong syringe?'

'Huh?'

'Is it possible he used your syringe?'

'No. I know the feel of mine. No, it's impossible. I shot up with my own syringe.'

'What about when you left?'

'I don't know what you're saying, Dad.'

'Could you have left your syringe there and taken Annabelle's by accident?'

'I don't see how. Right after we shot up, Annabelle . . . now wait a minute, you're getting me mixed up.'

'What happened exactly?'

'Well, we fixed ourselves, and I guess we put the syringes down. Yes, yes. Then Annabelle saw he was about to nod, so he got up and took his syringe and put it in his jacket pocket.'

'Were you watching him closely?'

'No. I only remember he was blowing his nose – addicts always got colds, you know – and then he remembered the spike, and he went over to get it and put it in his pocket. So that was when I went over for mine, too.'

'And you were high at the time?'

'Yeah.'

'Then you could have taken the wrong spike? The one Annabelle had been handling? Leaving your own spike behind?'

'I guess so, but . . .'

'Where's your syringe now?'

'On me.'

'Look at it.'

Larry reached into his pocket. He turned the syringe over in his hands studying it. 'It looks like mine,' he said.

'Is it?'

'It's hard to tell. Why? I don't get it.'

'There are some things you should know, Larry. First, Hernandez did not hang himself. He died of an overdose of heroin.'

'What? What?'

'Second, there was one and only one syringe found in the room with him.'

'Well, that figures. He . . .'

'The man who called me is after something. I don't know what yet. He said he'd call me again after I talked with you. He said you and Hernandez argued that afternoon. He says he has a witness who will swear to it. He says you were alone with Hernandez all that night. He says . . .'

'Me? Hell, I didn't argue with Annabelle. He laid a fix on me free, didn't he? Does that sound like we argued? How does this guy know all about this, anyway? Jesus, Dad . . .'

'Larry . . .'

'Who is this guy?'

'I don't know. He didn't give his name.'

'Well . . . well, let me get his witness! I didn't argue with Annabelle. We were friendly as hell. What's he trying to say, anyway? Is he trying to say I gave Annabelle that overdose? Is that what? Let him get his goddamn witness, go ahead, let him.'

'He doesn't need a witness, son.'

'No? I suppose a judge is just going to . . .'

'The man who called me said we'd find *your* fingerprints on the syringe in that basement room.'

CHAPTER NINE

AT three o'clock that morning, Maria Hernandez was ready to call it a day. She had thirty-five dollars in her purse, and she was tired, and it was cold, and if she fixed herself now and then went straight to sleep, she'd be set for the night. There was nothing like a nice warm fix before hitting the sack. For Maria, a shot of heroin was something that attacked her entire body. It made her tingle everywhere, even in what the Vice Squad and she herself referred to as her 'privates'.

The euphemistic use of the word by members of the Vice Squad was prescribed by law, since that law demanded that no arrest for prostitution could be made by a detective posing as a prospective client until the alleged prostitute's 'privates' had been exposed. Whether or not Maria had picked up the term from her Vice Squad associates, or whether it was a modestly maiden expression she herself had invented was a question for debate. She did have a good many Vice Squad associates – with some of whom she had going business arrangements, and with others of whom she had got into trouble. The trouble had been either of a legal-sexual nature or a socio-sexual nature. The Vice Squad because of its unique pincerlike position was thought of by many prostitutes as the Vise Squad. Again, this was a euphemism.

There were many euphemisms in Maria's business. She could discuss sex the way most other women discuss the latest fashion trends, except that Maria's discussion would have been far more coldly dispassionate. But she *could* discuss sex and generally did in no uncertain terms with other women in her trade. She discussed sex differently with men.

A man seeking her body was, when she discussed him with the other prostitutes, a 'john'. But in the polite society of a brew shared between male and female in a polite neighbourhood bistro, Maria invariably referred to a client as a 'friend'.

When Maria said, 'I have some very important friends,' she

did not mean she could have a speeding ticket fixed. She simply meant that many of the men who, euphemistically, slept with her were perhaps both wealthy and respected.

Nor would Maria ever stoop to describing in a vulgar manner the services she performed. Maria never 'slept' with a man. Maria, euphemistically, 'stayed with a friend'.

Whatever she did, and for whomever, she did it with a strangely detached attitude. There were, she realized, a good many more respectable ways of earning money. But Maria needed about forty dollars a day to feed her habit, and girls of Maria's age – unless they were movie stars – simply didn't earn that kind of money. It seemed provident to her that she had come fully equipped with a readily marketable commodity. And, following the age-old hand-in-glove practicality of supply and demand, she dutifully set about supplying whenever there was a demand.

There was a demand for Maria.

The suburban housewives, knitting and sewing, secure in the golden circle of their own wedding bands, would have been surprised to learn just how much of a demand there was for Maria. They might, in all truth, have been shocked.

For Maria had a good many friends who enjoyed the innocent, high-school-girl look about her. Being with Maria was like being a boy again, and even suburban housewives know that every man is just a little boy grown up. Maria's friends ranged from wealthy executives to file clerks, and her places of assignation ran the gamut from plush-lined private offices to blankets thrown on a factory floor. When she operated within the confines of the 87th Precinct, she generally enjoyed the rental of a room supplied at the rate of $3 per friend. The rooms were rented by various and sundry people, but usually by old women who derived their sole sources of income from such rentals. Maria did not enjoy working uptown. Her prices, because of the clientele, had to be lower there, and that meant entertaining more friends in order to accrue the boodle necessary for her daily drug requirement.

To say that Maria despised the sex act would be untrue. To say that she enjoyed it would be equally untrue. She neither enjoyed it nor despised it. She tolerated it. It was part of her job, and since there were many white-collar workers in the city who neither despised nor enjoyed but simply tolerated their jobs, her attitude was understandable. Her tolerance was helped by the peculiar ability of narcotics to quell the normal sex appetite. So, armed with the double-barrelled shotgun of under-stimulation through narcotics and indifference through prostitution, Maria stalked her game and quite miraculously led the game to consider her a hot-blooded huntress.

Her stalking, by three o'clock in the morning, left her a little weary. She had thirty-five dollars in her purse, and an eighth of heroin in her hotel room, and hell, it was time to call it a day. But thirty-five dollars was not forty dollars, and forty dollars was what Maria needed for her next day's supply, and so her relief at the day's work being over was partially clouded by a reluctance to quit when that additional five dollars was still lacking.

It was perhaps this reluctance that led to a chain of events that put her in the hospital.

She was walking with her head ducked against the wind, wearing high-heeled shoes and an unlined raincoat. She wore a smart blue silk skirt and white blouse under the raincoat. She had dressed in her best because she'd had a call downtown that afternoon, one of her important friends, and she'd hoped to cop the entire forty from him. But he'd been short on cash, and he'd asked her if it couldn't wait until next time, and knowing he had done this before, and knowing that payment had always followed the next time with perhaps a little bonus thrown in for her patience, Maria had smiled and said *certainly next time*, and then gone uptown to see what could be hustled. Dressed in her finery, she had managed very well. Still dressed in her finery, she headed now for the subway kiosk, anxious to get home for her fix, yet reluctant, but still anxious.

When she heard the footsteps behind her, she became a little frightened. Muggings were not uncommon uptown, and she didn't want to lose the thirty-five dollars she'd worked hard for all day. Her fright ebbed when a voice behind her whispered, 'Maria.'

She stopped, and then turned and waited, squinting into the wind. The man walked directly to her, grinning.

'Hello, Maria,' he said.

'Oh, you,' she said. 'Hello.'

'Where are you going?'

'Home,' she told him.

'So early?'

There was a lilt to his voice, and Maria had been in the business a long time, and whereas she had never been very fond of this particular man, and whereas she really did want to get home to that waiting fix, she nonetheless considered the five dollars or perhaps more which could just possibly be earned in a very short time, and she accepted the lilt in his voice and answered it with a mechanical smile.

'Well, it's not really as early as all that,' she said, still smiling, her voice somehow changed.

'Oh, sure,' he said, 'it's very early.'

'Well,' Maria answered, 'it depends on what you do with your time, I suppose.'

'I can think of a few things to do with the time,' he said.

'Can you?' She lifted one brow coquettishly and then moistened her lips.

'Yes, I can.'

'Well, I'm curious,' Maria said, stalking her game carefully now, knowing there was no joy to the hunt unless the hunted felt he was being chased. 'If it was early enough, and I'm not saying it is, but if it was, what would you like to do with the time?'

'I'd like to lay you, Maria,' he said.

'Oh now, that's vulgar,' Maria said.

'Is twenty dollars vulgar?' he asked, and suddenly Maria had no desire to play the game any more. Maria wanted that twenty dollars, the game be damned.

'All right,' she said quickly. 'Let me arrange for a room.'

'Do that,' he told her. She started away from him, and then she turned suddenly.

'I'm a one-way girl,' she warned him.

'Okay,' he said.

'I'll get the room.'

It was very late, she knew that, and perhaps she could not get a room for the usual three. But with twenty dollars promised, she could afford to risk five on a room, oh, this was wonderful, this was more than she could have hoped for. She climbed to the second flight of the tenement and knocked on one of the doors. At first, there was no answer, and so she knocked again, and then knocked repeatedly until a voice from within called, '*Basta! Basta!*' She recognized the 'Enoughs' as having erupted from the mouth of Dolores, and she grinned in the hallway, picturing the old woman getting out of bed. In a few moments, she heard the slap of bare feet approaching the doorway.

'*Quién es?*' a voice asked.

'Me,' she answered. 'Maria Hernandez.'

The door swung open. '*Puta!*' Dolores shouted. 'Why you break down the door at . . . *qué hora es?*'

Maria looked at her watch. '*Son las tres.* Look, Dolores, I need . . .'

Dolores stood in the doorway, a small thin woman in a faded nightgown, her grey hair straggly and hanging at the sides of her face, her collarbones showing sharply where the gown ended. The rage began building inside her, finally spread into her face, and then exploded from her mouth in a string of epithets. '*Puta!*' she screamed. '*Hija de la gran puta! Pendega! Cahapera!* Three o'clock in the morning, you come here and . . .'

'I need a room,' Maria said hastily. 'The one downstairs, is it . . . ?'

'*Bete para el carago!*' Dolores hurled, and she started to close the door.

'I can pay five dollars,' Maria said.

'*Me cago en los santos!*' Dolores went on, still cursing, and then the door stopped. '*Cinco?* You said five?'

'*Sí.*'

'The room downstairs is empty. I get the key. You stupid whore, why didn't you say five dollars? Come out of the hallway, you'll get pneumonia.'

Maria stepped into the apartment. In the kitchen, she could hear Dolores opening drawers, cursing mildly as she searched for the key. In a few moments, Dolores came back.

'The five,' she said.

Maria opened her purse and gave her five dollars. Dolores gave her the key. 'Good night,' Dolores said, and she closed the door.

He was still waiting in the street when Maria went to him. 'I got a room from Dolores,' she said.

'Who?'

'Dolores Faured. An old woman who ...' She stopped and grinned. 'Come,' she said, and she led him to a room at the rear of the ground floor. She opened the door, flicked on the wall light, and then locked the door behind him.

He reached for her almost instantly, and she danced away from him and said, 'I heard a proposal of twenty dollars.'

He took out his wallet, grinning. He was a big man with big hands, and she watched his hands, and she watched the methodical way in which he counted out the bills. He handed her the bills and because she didn't want to seem cheap – even though she'd already laid out five for the room – she didn't count them. She put them in her purse, and then took off her coat.

'Last time I saw you,' she said, 'you didn't seem interested in me personally. You were more interested in cards.'

'That was last time,' he said.

'Well, I'm not complaining,' she said.

'I've been looking for you all night,' he said.

'Really?' She walked toward him, wiggling suggestively. Now that the twenty dollars was in her purse, the game could proceed again. 'Well, you found me, baby.'

'I wanted to talk to you, Maria.'

'Come, baby, we'll talk horizontally,' she said.

'About Gonzo,' he told her.

'Gonzo?' She seemed puzzled. 'Oh, are you still saying that silly name?'

'I like it,' he said. 'Now, about your arrangement with Gonzo.'

'I have no arrangement with Gonzo,' she said. Slowly, she began unbuttoning her blouse.

'Ah, but you do.'

'Listen, is this all you want to do? Talk, I mean? You didn't have to pay me twenty dollars to talk.'

She took off the blouse and draped it over the back of a

71

chair. The chair, a bed, and a dresser were the only pieces of furniture in the room. He studied her and then said, 'You're small.'

'I'm not Jane Russell,' she answered, 'but I'm in proportion to the rest of me. For twenty dollars, you don't get movie queens.'

'I'm not complaining.'

'Then what's the holdup?'

'There's more to say first.'

Maria sighed. 'You want me to undress, or no?'

'In a minute.'

'This room ain't exactly warm, you know. Whatever I got, I don't want to freeze 'em.' She grinned, hoping he would grin back. He did not.

'About Gonzo,' he repeated.

'Gonzo, Gonzo, what's with you and Gonzo, anyway?'

'A lot,' he said. 'I asked Gonzo to make that arrangement with you.'

'Wha ...' She stared at him, surprised. 'You? You asked him to ...?'

'Me,' he said, and now he was grinning again.

Warily, she asked, 'What arrangement are you talking about?'

'The arrangement with Gonzo and your brother.'

'Go ahead,' she said, 'tell me more.'

'Where you promised Gonzo you'd swear you saw your brother and this Byrnes kid arguing.'

'Yeah?' she asked suspiciously.

'Yeah,' he answered. 'Gonzo was working on my orders. He gave you twenty-five dollars, didn't he?'

'Yes,' Maria said.

'And he said there'd be more, didn't he, if you swore you heard them arguing.'

'Yes,' Maria said. She shivered and said, 'I'm cold. I'm getting under the covers.' Unselfconsciously, she slipped out of her skirt, and then ran to the bed in her brassiere and panties and pulled the covers to her throat. 'Brrrrrrrr,' she said.

'Did Gonzo tell you what it was all about?'

'Only that this would be a good deal, and that my brother was in on it.'

'What about since your brother died? Has Gonzo said anything about that?'

'He said my brother fouled up the works. Listen, I'm cold, Come on over here.'

'Do you feel any differently about the deal since your brother died?' he asked, walking toward the bed. He took off his overcoat and draped it at the foot of the bed.

'No,' she said, 'why should I? He committed suicide. So why should . . .'

The man was grinning. 'Good,' he said. 'You keep thinking that way.'

'Sure,' she answered, puzzled by his grin. 'Why shouldn't I? The deal had nothing to do with Aníbal's death.'

'No,' he said. 'But just forget there ever was a deal, do you hear me? All you know is that your brother and this Byrnes kid argued, that's all. Do you understand? If anyone asks you – cops, reporters, anybody – that's your story.'

'Who is this Byrnes kid, anyway?' He was sitting on the bed now. 'Aren't you going to take off your clothes?' she asked.

'No, I'll leave them on.'

'Well, Jesus, I . . .'

'I'll leave them on.'

'All right,' she said quietly. She took his hand and guided it to her breast. 'Who is this Byrnes kid?'

'That doesn't matter. He argued with your brother.'

'Yes, yes, all right.' She was silent for a moment. 'Now, that's not so small, is it?'

'No,' he said.

'No,' she repeated. 'That's not so small at all, is it?' They were silent for several moments. He lay back on the bed, holding her.

'Remember,' he said again. '*Anyone* who asks you; cops, anyone.'

'I already spoke to one cop,' she said.

'Who?'

'I don't know his name. A good-looking one.'

'What did you tell him?'

'Nothing.'

'About the argument?'

'No. Gonzo said I should wait until I got the word on that. He said I should keep quiet until then. This cop . . .' She frowned.

'What?'

'He said . . . he said maybe Aníbal didn't commit suicide.'

'What did you say?'

Maria shrugged. 'He must have committed suicide.' She paused. 'Didn't he?'

'Sure, he did,' the man said. He held her tighter now. 'Maria . . .'

'No. No, wait. My brother. He . . . he didn't die because of this deal, did he? This deal had nothing to do with . . . I said *wait*!'

'I don't want to wait,' he told her.

'Did he commit suicide?' she asked, trying to hold him away from her.

'Yes. Yes, dammit, he committed suicide!'

'Then why are you so interested in making me lie to the cops? Was my brother killed? Was my . . . oh? Stop, you're hurting me!'

'Goddamn you, can't you shut your mouth!'

'Stop!' she said. 'Stop, please, you're hurting . . .'

'Then shut up about whether he was killed or he wasn't killed, who the hell gives a damn about that? What kind of a whore are you anyway?'

'He *was* killed, wasn't he?' she asked, bearing his weight now, the pain disappearing. 'Who killed him? Did you kill him?'

'No.'

'Did you?'

'Shut up! For Christ's sake, shut up!'

'Did you kill my brother? If you killed him, I'll never lie. If you killed him for one of your deals . . .' She felt something warm on the side of her face quite suddenly, but she didn't know what it was and so she kept talking. '. . . I'll go straight to the cops. He may have been a crumb, but he was my brother, and I'm not going to lie to . . .'

There was more warmth on her face, and then her throat.

She reached up suddenly and then, over his body, she studied her hand, and her eyes went wide with terror when she saw the blood. *He's cut me*, she thought. *Oh God Jesus, he's cut me!*

He backed away from her, arching his body, and she saw the knife in his right hand, the blade open, and then he slashed at her breasts and she rolled with all her strength, flinging him off her. He caught her arm and flung her back into the room, coming at her with the knife again. She held out her hands to ward off his blows, but he slashed, and then slashed back, and she began screaming as he continued swinging the knife, cutting the palms and fingers of her hands. She rushed to the door, groping with the lock, her fingers slashed, fumbling with the lock and unable to open it because her fingers would not do what she wanted them to do.

He swung her around, and she saw him pull back the knife, and then thrust forward with it, and she felt the blade when it tore skin just below her rib cage and then ripped across her body and slashed upwards. She fell back against the door, and he slashed at her neck and her face, and then he shouted, 'You don't have to lie for me, you bitch! You don't have to say another word, any more!' He threw her away from the door, and he unsnapped the lock, and then he scooped his coat from the bed, and went to her and stood staring at her for a moment, staring at the blood-smeared caricature that had once been Maria Hernandez, and then maliciously he thrust the knife deep into her breast and brought it across her body, sure he had struck her heart. He watched as she fell to the floor, and then he ran through the door and out of the building.

She lay in a pool of her own blood, thinking *He killed my brother and now he has killed me. He killed my brother because of his deal, I was to lie, I was to say Byrnes and Aníbal argued, Gonzo told me that, a good deal he said, he gave me twenty-five dollars, more to come, he killed my brother.*

And miraculously, she crawled to the open doorway, naked, running blood every inch of the way, and she crawled into the hallway, not screaming because there was no strength in her to scream with, crawling the long, long length of the hall-way while her life drained out of her, running red into the bare brown wooden floor of the building, and then into the entryway with its mailboxes, and she reached up and managed to hold the doorknob in her tattered fingers, and managed to twist the doorknob, and then fell face forward on to the sidewalk, still bleeding.

A patrolman named Alf Levine found her a half-hour later as he was making his round. He called an ambulance immediately.

CHAPTER TEN

THERE were four bulls in the Squad Room of the 87th on the night Maria Hernandez was stabbed.

Detectives Meyer and Willis were sitting at one of the desks, drinking coffee. Detective Bongiorno was typing up a D.D. report to be turned over to the Safe and Loft Squad. Detective Temple was sitting at the telephone, catching.

'I don't like coffee in containers,' Meyer said to Willis. Meyer was a Jew whose father had a hilarious sense of humour. And since Meyer had been a change-of-life baby, which, in a sense, had been a big practical joke on the old man, the old man had decided to play his own little joke on his son. And since his son's surname was Meyer, he could think of nothing more side-splitting than to make his son's given name Meyer, too. In those days, babies were born at home, delivered by midwives. There was none of the hospital pressure to name a child. Meyer's father withheld his choice of a name until the *briss*. He announced it just as the *moile* was performing the circumcision, and the resultant shock almost caused him to have a castrated son.

Fortunately, Meyer Meyer emerged intact, if not altogether triumphant. A name like Meyer Meyer is a difficult burden to bear, especially if you live in a neighbourhood where kids were wont to slit your throat if you happened to have blue eyes. Remarkably, considering the Meyer Meyer handle, and considering the unfortunate coincidence that had provided Meyer with blue eyes, he had managed to survive. He attributed his survival to an almost supernaturally patient attitude. Meyer Meyer was the most patient man in the world. But when a man bears the burden of a double-barrelled name, and when a man is raised as an Orthodox Jew in a predominantly Gentile neighbourhood, and when a man has made patience his credo, something's got to give. Meyer Meyer, though he was only thirty-seven years old, was as bald as a cue ball.

'It simply doesn't taste like coffee,' he expanded.

'No? Then what does it taste like?' Willis asked, sipping.

'It tastes like cardboard, if you want to know. Now, don't misunderstand me. I like cardboard. My wife often serves cardboard for dinner. She has some wonderful recipes for cardboard.'

'She must have got them from my wife,' Temple called over.

'Well,' Meyer said, 'you know how wives are. Always exchanging recipes. But my point is that I wouldn't want you to believe I'm prejudiced against cardboard. Not at all. In fact, I might honestly say that the taste of cardboard is a taste cultivated among gourmets and civilized humans all over the world.'

'Then what's your beef?' Willis asked, smiling.

'Expectancy,' Meyer said patiently.

'I don't get it,' Willis said.

'Hal, when my wife serves dinner, I *expect* the taste of cardboard. We have been married, God bless her, for twelve years now and she has never disappointed me on the matter of dinner. I expect the taste of cardboard, and it is the cardboard taste I get. But when I order coffee from the local luncheonette, my taste buds are geared to enjoy the tongue-tingling tang of coffee. As you might say, my face is fixed for coffee.'

'So?'

'So the disappointment, after the great expectations, is almost too great to bear. I order coffee, and I'm forced to drink cardboard.'

'Who's forcing you?' Willis asked.

'To tell you the truth,' Meyer said, 'I'm beginning to forget what coffee in a cup tastes like. Everything in my life tastes like cardboard now. It's a sad thing.'

'I'm weeping,' Temple said.

'There are compensations, I suppose,' Meyer said wearily.

'And what are they?' Willis asked, still smiling.

'A friend of mine has a wife who has cultivated the knack of making everything taste like sawdust.' Willis laughed aloud, and Meyer chuckled and then shrugged. 'I suppose cardboard is better than sawdust, already.'

'You should switch wives every now and then,' Temple advised. 'Break the monotony.'

'Of the meals, you mean?' Meyer asked.

'What else?' Temple said, shrugging grandly.

'Knowing your filthy mind,' Meyer began, and the telephone on Temple's desk rang. Temple lifted the receiver.

'87th Squad,' he said, 'Detective Temple.' He listened. The Squad Room was silent. 'Uh-huh,' he said. 'Okay, I'll send some men. Right.' He hung up. 'Knifing on South 14th,' he said. 'Levine's already called an ambulance. Meyer, Hal, you want to take this?'

Meyer went to the clothes rack and began shrugging into his coat. 'How come,' he wanted to know, 'you're always catching when it's cold outside?'

'What hospital?' Willis asked.

'General,' Temple said. 'Call in later, will you? This looks pretty serious.'

'How so?' Meyer asked.

'It may turn into a homicide.'

Meyer had never liked the smell of hospitals. His mother had died of cancer in a hospital, and he would always remember her pain-wracked face, and he would always remember the smells of sickness and death, the hospital smells that had invaded his nostrils and entrenched themselves there for ever.

He did not like doctors, either. His dislike of doctors probably had its origin in the fact that a doctor had originally diagnosed his mother's malignant cancer as a sebaceous cyst. But aside and apart from this indisputably prejudiced viewpoint, he also found doctors unbearably conceited and possessed of, to Meyer, a completely unwarranted sense of self-importance. Meyer was not a man to scoff at education. He himself was a college graduate who happened to be a cop. A medical man was a college graduate who happened to have a doctorate. The doctorate, in Meyer's mind, simply meant four years of additional schooling. These years of schooling, necessary before a physician could begin practice, were akin to the years of apprenticeship any man had to serve in any given field before he became a success in that field. Why then did most doctors feel superior to, for example, advertising men? Meyer would never understand it.

He supposed it broke down to the basic drive for survival. A doctor allegedly held survival in his hands. Meyer's impression, however, was that the physicians had inadvertently and quite unconsciously correctly labelled the pursuit of their chosen profession: practice. As far as Meyer was concerned, all doctors were doing just that: practising. And until they got perfect, he would stay away from them.

Unfortunately, the intern in whose hands the life of Maria Hernandez lay did not help to raise Meyer's opinion of medical men in general.

He was a young boy with bright blond hair clipped close to his scalp. His eyes were brown, and his features were regular, and he looked very handsome and very clean in his hospital tunic. He also looked very frightened. He had perhaps seen cut-up cadavers in medical school, but Maria Hernandez was the first live person he'd seen so mutilated. He stood in the hospital corridor, puffing nervously on a cigarette, talking to Meyer and Willis.

'What's her condition now?' Willis asked.

'Critical,' the young doctor said.

'How critical? How much longer has she got?'

'That's ... that's hard to say. She's ... she's very badly cut. We've ... we've managed to stop the blood, but there was so much loss before she got to us ...' The doctor swallowed. 'It's hard to say.'

'May we talk to her, Doctor Fredericks?' Meyer asked.

'I ... I don't think so.'

'*Can* she talk?'

'I ... I don't know.'

'For Christ's sake, pull yourself together!' Meyer said irritably.

'I beg your pardon?' Fredericks said.

79

'If you have to vomit, go ahead,' Meyer said. 'Then come back and talk sensibly.'

'What?' Fredericks said. 'What?'

'All right, listen to me,' Meyer said very patiently. 'I know you're in charge of this great big shining hospital, and you're probably the world's foremost brain surgeon, and a little Puerto Rican girl bleeding her guts out over your floors is an inconvenience. But –'

'I didn't say –'

'*But*,' Meyer continued, 'it so happens that someone stabbed that little girl, and our job is to find whoever did it so that it won't happen again and cause you further inconvenience. A dying declaration is competent evidence. If the person has no hope of recovery, and if we get a declaration, the courts will admit it. Now – is that little girl going to live, or isn't she?'

Fredericks seemed stunned.

'Is she?'

'I don't think so.'

'Then may we talk to her?'

'I would have to check that.'

'Well then, would you please, for the love of God, go check it?'

'Yes. Yes, I'll do that. You understand, the responsibility is not mine. I couldn't grant permission for questioning the girl without check –'

'Go, go, already,' Meyer said. 'Check. Hurry.'

'Yes,' Fredericks said, and he hurried off down the corridor in a fury of sudden starched energy.

'You know the questions we're supposed to ask?' Willis said. 'To make this admissible?'

'I think so. You want to run over them?'

'Yeah, we'd better. I think we should get a stenographer up here, too.'

'Depends on how much time there is. Maybe there's a loose secretary hanging around the hospital. A police stenographer would take –'

'No, not enough time for that. We'll ask Fredericks if someone can take shorthand. Think she'll be able to sign?'

'I don't know. What about the questions?'

'The name and the address first,' Willis said.

'Yes. Then, *Do you now believe that you are about to die*?'

'Yeah,' Willis said. 'What comes next?'

'Jesus, I hate this, you know?' Meyer said.

'Something about *Do you hope to recover . . .*?'

'No, no, it's *Have you no hope of recovery from the effects of the injury you have received*?' Meyer shook his head. 'Jesus, I hate this.'

'And then the business about *Are you willing to make a true statement of how you received the injury from which you are now suffering*? That's all of it, isn't it?'

'Yes,' Meyer said. 'Jesus, that little girl in there . . .'

'Yeah,' Willis said. Both men fell silent. They could hear the quiet *thrum* of the hospital all around them, like a giant white heart pumping blood. In a little while, they heard footsteps echoing down the corridor.

'Here's Fredericks now,' Willis said.

Dr Fredericks approached them. He was sweating, and his tunic looked rumpled and soiled.

'How about it?' Meyer said. 'Did you get us permission?'

'It doesn't matter,' Fredericks said.

'Huh?'

'The girl is dead.'

CHAPTER ELEVEN

BECAUSE the room in which Maria Hernandez kept her fatal assignation with a person or persons unknown was the last known place to have enclosed her murderer, it was open to particular scrutiny by the police.

This scrutiny was of a non-theoretical nature. The laboratory technicians who descended upon the premises were not interested in exercising their imaginations. They were interested solely in clues that might lead to the identity of the person or persons who had wantonly slashed and murdered the Hernandez girl. They were looking for facts. And so, after the room had been sketched and photographed, they got down to business, and their business was a slow and laborious one.

Chance impressions are, of course, fingerprints.

The three kinds of chance impressions are:

1. Latent prints – these are invisible. Sometimes they can be picked up with the naked eye unaided, provided they are on a smooth surface and provided indirect lighting is used.
2. Visible prints – which happen to be visible only because the person who left them behind was a slob. And, being a slob, he'd allowed his fingers to become smeared with something containing colour. The colour was usually provided by dirt or blood.
3. Plastic prints – which, as the definition implies, are left in some sort of a plastic material like putty, wax, tar, clay, or the inside of a banana peel.

Naturally, plastic prints and visible prints are the nicest kinds of chance impressions to find. At least, they entail the least amount of location work. But chance impressions being what they are – that is, fingerprints inadvertently and unconsciously left behind – the person leaving them is not always so considerate as to leave the easiest kind to find. Most chance impressions are latent prints, and latent prints must be made visible through the use of fine-grained, lumpless powders before they can be photographed or transferred on foils. This takes time. The lab boys had a lot of time, and they also had a lot of latents to play around with. The room in which Maria Hernandez had been slashed, you see, was a room used to the steady going and coming of men. Patiently, slowly, the lab boys dusted and dusted, and photographed and transferred, coming up with a total of ten different men who had left good clear latents around the room.

They did not know that none of these men was the one who'd killed Maria. They could not have known that Maria's murderer had worn gloves until he'd climbed into bed with her that night. They did not know, and so they passed the prints on to the detectives, who checked them through I.B. and then indulged in a time-consuming roundup of available possible killers, all of whom had readily accessible (and generally true) alibis. Some of the prints had been left by persons who had never had a brush with the police. The I.B. could not identify those prints. Those men were never pulled in for questioning.

Considering the nature of the murder room, the lab boys were not surprised to find a good many naked footprints here and there, especially in the dust-covered corners near the bed. Unfortunately, the I.B. did not keep an active footprint file. These footprints then were simply put away for possible comparison with suspects later on. One of the footprints, unsurprisingly, had been left by Maria Hernandez.

The lab boys could find no usable shoe impressions in the room.

They found many head hairs and several pubic hairs on the bloodstained sheets of the bed. They also found semen stains. The blanket that had been on the bed was vacuumed, and the dust collected on filter paper. The dust was then examined and analysed carefully. The technicians found nothing in the dust that proved helpful to them.

They found one thing in the room that was of possible real value.

A feather.

Now, the work they performed in that room may sound very simple and very unstrenuous, especially when all they could turn up was a lousy little feather, a handful of unimportant latents, and a few soleprints, and some hairs, and some blood, and some semen.

Really now! How much work could all that have involved?

Well, a semen stain looks like a geographical map and has the feel of a starched area. Unfortunately, looks alone are not enough for the purposes of identification. The suspected stain had to be packed. It had to be packed so that no friction ensued, because semen stains are brittle and can fracture into tiny, easily lost pieces. Friction could also break the spermatozoa. In other words, the stain could not be rolled, and it could not be folded, and it could not be haphazardly tossed into a bag of old clothes. It had to be packed so that its sides were absolutely free of friction of any sort, and this took time and trouble.

When the suspect stain reached the laboratory, its real examination began.

The first microchemical test it underwent was called the Florence reaction test, wherein a small part of the stain was dissolved in a solution of 1.56 grammes of iodide of potassium, 2.54 grammes of pure crystalline iodine, and 30 c.c. of distilled water. The test showed only that there was a probability of semen in the stain. It showed this because brown and rhombic-shaped Florence semen crystals appeared under the microscope. Unfortunately, however, similar crystals could have been obtained with either mucus or saliva, and so the test was not conclusive. But it did admit to a probability, and so the second test was performed, and the second test was the Puranen reaction test.

The Puranen reagent, into which a part of the stain extracted with several drops of saline was placed, consisted of a five-per-cent solution of 2, 4-dinitro-1-naphthol-7-sulphonic acid, flavianic acid. The stain portion, the saline, and the solution were put into a micro tube, and the tube in turn put into a refrigerator for several hours. At the end of that time a yellowish precipitate of spermine flavianate was visible at the bottom of the tube. This precipitate was put under the microscope, and the all-powerful eye revealed crosslike crystals characteristic of seminal fluid.

And then, of course, the further microscopic examination included a search for at least several spermheads – defined by shape and staining – with necks attached. Luckily, the stain had not been changed by either friction or putrefaction. Had it been so altered, the search for the presence of spermatozoa might have been even more time-consuming and less fruitful.

So that's what they did with one stain. It consumed the major part of the day. Nor was it very exciting work. They were not searching for elusive cold germs. They were not seeking the cure for cancer. They were simply trying to compile a list of facts that might lead to the killer of Maria Hernandez or that, at a later date, might help to identify a suspect positively.

And if these men devoted long hours to the death of one junkie, another man was devoting long hours to the life of another junkie.

The junkie happened to be his son.

Peter Byrnes would never know how close he had come to washing his hands of the whole matter. He had fought first with the idea that the entire concept was a hoax. *My son a drug addict?* he had asked, *my son? My son's fingerprints on an alleged murder weapon?* No, he had told himself, it is a lie, a complete lie from start to finish. He would seek out this lie, pull it from beneath its rock, force it to crawl into the sunshine where he could step upon it. He would confront his son with the lie, and together they would destroy it.

But he had confronted his son, and he had known even before he asked 'Are you a drug addict?' that his son was indeed a drug addict, and that a portion of the lie was not a lie. The knowledge had at once shocked and disgusted him, even though he had somehow expected it. For a lesser man than Byrnes, for a lesser cop than Byrnes, the knowledge might have beeen less devastating. But Byrnes despised crime, and Byrnes despised punks, and he had learned that his son was a punk engaged in criminal activities. And they had faced each other in their silent living-room, and Byrnes had talked logically and sensibly, Byrnes had outlined the entire predicament to his son, never once allowing his disgust to rise into his throat, never once crying out against this punk criminal who was his son, never once saying the words of banishment.

His instinct told him to throw this person out into the street. This was an instinct nurtured over the years, an instinct that was an ingrained part of Byrnes's character.

But there was a deeper instinct, an instinct shared at fires in paleolithic times, when men clasped sons against the night, and the instinct had been passed down through the blood of man, and it coursed through the veins of Peter Byrnes, and Byrnes could think only *He is my son.*

And so he had talked levelly and calmly, exploding only once or twice, but even then exploding only with impatience and not allowing the disgust to overrule his mind.

His son was an addict.

Irrevocably, irreconcilably, his son was an addict. The caller had not lied on that score.

The second half of the lie turned out to be true, too. Byrnes checked his son's fingerprints against those that had been found on the syringe, and the fingerprints matched. He revealed this information to no one in the department, and the concealment left him feeling guilty and somehow contaminated.

The lie, then, had not been a lie at all.

It had started out as a two-part falsehood, and had turned into a shining, shimmering truth.

But what about the rest? Had Larry argued with Hernandez on the afternoon of the boy's death? And if he had, were not the implications clear? Were not the implications that Larry Byrnes had killed Aníbal Hernandez perfectly clear?

Byrnes could not believe the implications.

His son had turned into something he could not easily understand, something he had perhaps never understood and might never understand – but he knew his son was not a murderer.

And so, on that Thursday, 21 December, he waited for the man to call again, as he had promised; and he bore the additional burden now of a new homicide, the death of Aníbal's sister. He waited all that day, and no call came, and when he went home in the afternoon, it was to a task he dreaded.

He liked a happy home, but there was no joy in his house now. Harriet met him in the hallway, and she took his hat, and then she went into his arms, and she sobbed against his shoulder, and he tried to remember the last time she had cried like this, and it seemed very long ago, and he could not remember except that it was somehow attached to a senior prom and a corsage, and the insurmountable problems of an eighteen-year-old girl. Harriet wasn't eighteen any more. She had a son who was almost eighteen now, and that son's problem had nothing to do with senior proms or corsages.

'How is he?' Byrnes asked.

'Bad,' Harriet said.

'What did Johnny say?'

'He's given him something as a substitute,' Harriet answered. 'But he's only a doctor, Peter, he said that, he said he's only a doctor and the boy has to *want* to break the habit. Peter, how did this happen? For God's sake, how did it happen?'

'I don't know,' Byrnes said.

'I thought this was for slum kids. I thought it was for kids who came from broken homes, kids who didn't have love. How did it happen to Larry?'

And again, Byrnes said, 'I don't know,' and within himself he condemned the job that had not left him more time to devote to his only son. But he was too honest to level the entire blame on the job, and he reminded himself that other men had jobs with long hours, irregular hours, and their sons did not become drug addicts. And so he started up the steps to his son's room, walking heavily, suddenly grown old, and beneath his own feelings of guilt ran the pressing undercurrent of his disgust. His son was a junkie. The word blinked like a neon sign in his head: JUNKIE. Junkie. JUNKIE. Junkie.

He knocked on his son's door.

'Larry?'

'Dad? Open this, will you? For Christ's sake, open it.'

Byrnes reached into his pocket and took out his key ring. He had locked Larry into his room only once that he could remember. The boy had broken a plate-glass window with a baseball and then flatly refused to pay for the damage out of his allowance. Byrnes had informed his son that he would then deduct the money from the meals Larry ate, and that all meals would stop as of that moment. He had put the boy in the room and locked the door from the outside, and Larry had capitulated shortly after dinner that night. The incident, at the time, had not seemed terribly important. A form of punishment and really, really now, if Larry had still refused, Byrnes would certainly have fed him. Byrnes had felt, at the time, that he was teaching his son a respect for other people's property as well as a respect for money. But now, looking back, he wondered if he had not behaved wrongly. Had he isolated his son's affection by punishing him in that way? Had his son automatically assumed there was no love for him in this house? Had his son assumed Byrnes was taking the side of the shopkeeper and not that of his own flesh and blood?

But what is a man supposed to do? Consult a psychology

textbook before he says anything or does anything? And how many other small incidents were there, how many incidents over the years, how many incidents piling up, inconsequential in themselves, gathering force and power as they accumulated until, together, they conspired to force a boy into drug addiction? How many incidents, and for how many of them could a father be blamed? Was he a bad father? Didn't he truly and honestly love his son, and hadn't he always tried to do what was best for him, hadn't he always tried to raise his son as a decent human being? What is a man supposed to do, what is a man supposed to do?

He unlocked the door, and then stepped into the room.

Larry stood just before the bed, his fists clenched.

'Why am I a prisoner?' he shouted.

'You're not a prisoner,' Byrnes said calmly.

'No? Then what is it when the door's locked? What the hell, am I a criminal or something?'

'To be technical, yes, you are.'

'Dad, listen, don't play games with me today. I'm not in any goddamn mood to be playing games.'

'You were found by a law-enforcement officer to be carrying a hypodermic syringe. That's against the law. That law-enforcement officer also found an eighth of an ounce of heroin in your dresser drawer, and that's against the law. So you are, in effect, a criminal, and I am aiding and abetting you – so shut up, Larry.'

'Don't tell me to shut up, Dad. What was that crap your friend gave me?'

'What?'

'Your big friend. Your big-shot doctor friend. He's probably never seen an addict in his whole life. What'd you drag him in for? What makes you think I need him? I told you I could drop the stuff any time I wanted to, didn't I? So what'd you have to call him in for? I hate that son of a bitch.'

'He happened to bring you into the world, Larry.'

'So what am I supposed to do? Give him a medal or something? He got paid for the delivery, didn't he?'

'He's a friend, Larry.'

'Then why'd he tell you to lock me in my room?'

'Because he doesn't want you to leave this house. You're sick.'

'Oh, Jesus, I'm sick. I'm sick, all right. I'm sick of everybody's attitude around here. I told you I'm not hooked! Now what do I have to do to prove it?'

'You're hooked, Larry,' Byrnes said quietly.

'I'm hooked, I'm hooked, I'm hooked, is that the only goddamn song you know? Is that the only one you and your bigshot doctor friend rehearsed? Jesus Christ, how'd I ever get such a goddamn square for a father?'

'I'm sorry I disappoint you,' Byrnes said.

'Oh boy, here we go. Here comes the martyred-fatherhood routine! I saw this in the movies ever since I was eight. Turn it off, Pop, it doesn't reach me.'

'I'm not trying to reach you,' Byrnes said. 'I'm trying to cure you.'

'How? With that crap your friend gave me? What was that crap, anyway?'

'A substitute drug of some sort.'

'Yeah? Well, it's no damn good. I feel exactly the same. You could have saved your money. Listen, you want to do me a real favour? You really want to cure me?'

'You know I do.'

'All right, go out and scare me up some junk. There must be plenty of it down at the station house. Listen, I got a better idea. Give me back that eighth you took from my dresser.'

'No.'

'Why not? Dammit, you just said you wanted to help me! Okay, so why won't you help me? Don't you want to help me?'

'I want to help you.'

'Then get me the stuff.'

'No.'

'You big son of a bitch,' Larry said, and the tears suddenly started on his face. 'Why don't you help me? Get out of here! Get out of here! Get out of here, you lousy ...' and the sentence dissolved into a series of animal sobs.

'Larry ...'

'Get out!' Larry shrieked.

'Son ...'

'Don't call me your son! Don't call me that! What the hell do you care about me? You're just afraid you'll lose your cushy job because I'm a junkie, that's all.'

'That's not true, Larry.'

'It *is* true! You're scared crap because you think somebody'll find out about my habit and about those fingerprints on the syringe! Okay, you bastard, okay, you just wait 'til I get to a telephone.'

'You're not getting to a phone until you're cured, Larry.'

'That's what you think! When I get to a phone, I'm gonna call the newspapers, and I'm gonna tell them all about it. Now, how about that? How about it, Dad? HOW ABOUT IT? Do I get that eighth?'

'You're not getting the heroin, and you're not getting near a phone, either. Now relax, son.'

'*I don't want to relax!*' Larry shouted. 'I *can't* relax! Listen, you! Now listen to me, you! Now you just listen to me!' He stood facing his father, his face streaked with tears, his eyes red, pointing his finger up at his father's face, shaking the finger as if it were a dagger. 'Now listen to me! I want that stuff, do you hear me? Now you get that stuff for me, do you hear?'

'I hear you. You're not getting any heroin. If you want me to, I'll call John again.'

'I don't want your snotnose doctor here again!'

'He's going to keep treating you until you're cured, Larry.'

'Cured of *what*? Can't you get it through your head that I'm not sick? What's he going to cure?'

'If you're not sick, why do you want a shot?'

'To tide me over, you damn jerk!'

'Over what?'

'Until I'm okay again. Dammit, do I have to spell everything out? What's the matter, are you stupid? I thought you were a cop, I thought cops were supposed to be smart!'

'I'll call Johnny,' Byrnes said. He turned and started for the door.

'*No!*' Larry screamed. 'I don't want him here again! That's it! That's final! Now that's it!'

'He might be able to lessen your pain.'

'What pain? Don't talk to me about pain. What do you

90

know about pain? You've been living all your stupid life, and you don't know half the pain I know. I'm eighteen, and I know more pain than you'll ever know. So don't tell me about pain. *You don't know pain, you bastard!*'

'Larry, do you want me to knock you down?' Byrnes asked quietly.

'What? What? You going to hit me? Okay, go ahead. Be a big muscle man, what the hell will that get you? You going to beat me out of this?'

'Out of what?'

'Out of what, out of what, I don't know what! Oh, you're a tricky bastard. You're trying to get me to say I'm sick, ain't you? You're trying to get me to say I'm hooked, I know. I know. Well, *I'm not!*'

'I'm not trying to get you to say anything.'

'No, huh? Well then, go ahead, why don't you beat me? Why don't you make believe this is your squad room, go ahead, start using your fists, start beating me up. You can take me easy. You can ...' He stopped suddenly and clutched at his stomach. He stood doubled over, his arm crossing his middle. Byrnes watched him helplessly.

'Larry ...'

'Shhh,' Larry said softly.

'Son, what ... ?'

'Shhhh, shhhh.' He stood rocking on his heels, back and forth, clutching his stomach, and then finally he lifted his head, and his eyes were wet, and this time the tears coursed down his face, and he said, 'Dad, I'm sick, I'm very sick.'

Byrnes went to him and put his arm around his shoulder. He tried to think of something comforting to say, but nothing would come to his tongue.

'Dad, I'm asking you, please. Please, Dad, would you please get me something? Dad, please, I'm very sick, and need a fix. So please, Dad, please, I'm begging you, get me something. Please get me something, just a little bit to tide me over, please, Dad, please. I'll never, never ask you for anything else as long as I live. I'll leave home, I'll do whatever you say, but please get me something, Dad. If you love me, please get me something.'

'I'll call Johnny,' Byrnes said.

'No, Dad, please, please, that stuff he gave me is no good, it doesn't help.'

'He'll try something else.'

'No, please, please, please, please. . . .'

'Larry, Larry, son . . .'

'Dad, if you love me . . .'

'I love you, Larry,' Byrnes said, and he held his son's shoulder tightly, and there were tears on his own face now, and his son shuddered and then said, 'I have to go to the bathroom. I have to . . . Dad, help me, help me.'

And Byrnes took his son to the bathroom across the hall, and Larry was very sick. At the foot of the stairs, Harriet stood with her hands wrung together, and after a while her husband and her son crossed the hall again, and then Byrnes came out of Larry's bedroom and locked the door on the outside and went down the steps to his wife.

'Call Johnny again,' he said. 'Tell him to get right over.'

Harriet hesitated, and her eyes were on Byrnes's face, and Byrnes said, 'He's very sick, Harriet. He's really very sick.'

Harriet, with the wisdom of a wife and mother, knew that this was not what Byrnes wanted to say at all. She nodded and went to the telephone.

The lions were really kicking it up.

Maybe they're hungry, Carella thought. Maybe they'd like a nice fat detective for dinner. It's a pity I'm not a fat detective, but maybe they're not very choosy lions, maybe they'll settle for a lean detective.

I am certainly a lean detective.

I have been leaning against this stupid cage since 2 p.m., and waiting for a man named Gonzo whom I have never seen in my life. I have been leaning and leaning, and the lions are roaring inside the building, and it is now 4.37, and my good friend Gonzo or anything resembling my good friend Gonzo has still not appeared.

And even when he does appear, he may not be very important at all. Except for the fact that he's a pusher, and it's always nice to grab another pusher. But he may not be important in the Hernandez case, even though he seems to have inherited at least some of the boy's customers, God, the girl! God, the job somebody did on that poor girl! Was it because of her brother?

What, what?

What is it? What's behind such a fishy goddamn suicide? It looks like a suicide set-up, but it's obviously not a suicide set-up, and whoever killed that boy knew that, whoever killed that boy wanted us to know it was *not* a suicide! He wanted us to dig deeper, and he wanted us to come up with a homicide, but why? And whose fingerprints are on that syringe? Do they belong to this Gonzo character I'm now waiting for, a nice grubby pusher who hasn't got a record? Are they his prints and will we find out what this whole goddamn mess is about the minute we get him? And is he the one who slashed the girl to ribbons or was that something separate and apart, something that just happened to a prostitute, an occupational hazard, something not at all connected with the earlier death of her brother?

Will Gonzo know the answers?

And if you know the answers, Mr Gonzo, or Gonzo Mr, because I don't know whether Gonzo is your first name or your last name, you certainly have kept yourself well hidden in this precinct, you certainly have operated on a small quiet scale, but if you know the answers where the hell are you now?

Have you been operating before this, Gonzo?

Or did you suddenly inherit a nice business the night you knocked off Aníbal Hernandez? Was that why you killed him?

But what kind of a business did the kid have, when you really examined it closely? Kling beat that whole neighbourhood with his feet, and he scared up a handful of Hernandez's erstwhile customers. A mule, pure and simple, shoving only enough stuff to keep him in the junk himself. So is a business of such minuscule size a reason for murder? Do people kill for a handful of pennies?

Well, yes, people *do* kill for a handful of pennies sometimes.

But usually the pennies are in plain sight, and the pennies are the temptation. Hernandez's business was a non-tangible thing, and if he were killed for that business then why, why in Christ's holy name, had the killer gone out of his way to indicate homicide?

Because surely the killer must have known that death by overdose could have been suicide. Had he left the body where it lay, syringe on the cot next to it, chances are a suicide verdict would have been delivered. The coroner would have examined the boy and said *yes, death by overdose*, as he had in fact said. Aníbal Hernandez would have been chalked off as a careless junkie. But the killer had affixed that rope to the kid's neck, and the rope had been placed there after the boy was dead, and surely the killer *knew* this would draw suspicion, surely the killer knew that. He had wanted suspicion of homicide.

Why?

And where is Gonzo?

Carella took a bag of peanuts out of his pocket. He was wearing grey corduroy slacks, and a grey suède jacket. He wore, too, black loafers and bright red socks. The socks were a mistake. He realized that after he'd left the house. The socks stood out like lights on a Christmas tree, God, what was he going to get Teddy for Christmas? He had seen some nice lounging pyjamas, but she'd murder him if he spent $25.00 for lounging pyjamas. Still, they would look beautiful on her, everything looked beautiful on her, why shouldn't a man be allowed to spend $25.00 on the woman he loved? She had told him with her lips that his love was enough, that he himself was the biggest and best Christmas present she had ever received, and that anything in excess of $15.00 worth of merchandise would be the silliest sort of extravagance for a girl who already had the nicest gift in the world. She had told him this, and he had held her close, but dammit, those lounging pyjamas were still very pretty, and he could visualize her wearing them, so what the devil was an additional $10.00 when you got right down to it? How many people threw away $10.00 every day of the week without giving it a second thought.

Carella popped a peanut into his mouth.

Where was Gonzo?

Probably doing Christmas shopping, Carella thought. Do pushers have wives and mothers, too? Of course they do. And of course they exchange Christmas gifts and they go to baptisms and bar-mitzvahs and weddings and funerals just like every-body else. So maybe Gonzo *is* doing his Christmas shopping, the idea isn't such a far-fetched one at that. I wish *I* were doing *my* Christmas shopping right now instead of munching on stale peanuts in this bitter cold outside the lion house. Besides, I don't like working outside my own precinct. All right, that's an idiosyncrasy, and I'm a crazy cop, but there's no place like home, and this park belongs to two other precincts, none of which is the 87th, and I like the 87th, and that makes me a crazier cop, have another peanut, idiot.

Come on, Gonzo.

I'm dying to make your acquaintance, Gonzo. I've heard so much about you that I feel I actually know you, and really, hasn't our meeting been postponed for just an unbearably long time? Come on, Gonzo. I am beginning to resemble the brass monkeys, Gonzo. I'd like very much to go inside and look at the lions – how come they're so quiet now? Feeding time already? – and toast myself by their cages rather than stand out here where even my red socks are turning blue from the cold. So how about it, Gonzo? Give a flatfoot a break, will you? Give a poor honest cop a dime for a cup of coffee, willya? Oh brother, would I love a hot cup of coffee right this minute, mmmmm.

I'll bet you're having a cup of coffee in some department-store restaurant right now, Gonzo. I'll bet you don't even know I'm here waiting for you.

Hell, I sure hope you *don't* know I'm waiting for you.

Carella cracked open another peanut and then glanced casually at a young boy who turned the corner of the lion house. The boy looked at Carella and then walked past. Carella seemingly ignored him, munching happily and idiotically on his peanuts. When the boy was gone, Carella moved to one of the benches and sat, waiting. He glanced at his watch. He cracked open another peanut. He glanced at his watch again.

In three minutes, the boy was back. He was no older than nineteen. He walked with a quick, birdlike tempo. He wore a sports jacket, the collar turned up against the cold, and a pair of shabby grey flannel slacks. His head was bare, and his blond hair danced in the wind. He looked at Carella again, and then went to stand near the outdoor cages of the lion house. Carella seemed interested only in cracking open and eating his peanuts. He barely gave the boy a glance, but the boy was never out of his sight.

The boy was pacing now. He looked at his wrist, and then seemingly remembered he didn't have a watch. He pulled a grimace, glanced up the path, and then began pacing in front of the cages again. Carella went on eating his peanuts.

The boy suddenly stopped pacing, stood undecided for a moment, and then walked over to where Carella was sitting.

'Hey, mister,' he said, 'you know what time it is?'

'Just a second,' Carella answered. He finished cracking a peanut, popped it into his mouth, put the shell on to the little pile he'd formed on the bench, dusted his hands, and then looked at his watch.

'About a quarter to five,' he said.

'Thanks,' the boy answered. He looked off up the path again. He turned back to Carella and studied him for a minute. 'Pretty cold, ain't it?' he said.

'Yeah,' Carella answered. 'Want a peanut?'

'Huh? Oh, no. Thanks.'

'Good,' Carella said. 'Give you some energy, build body warmth.'

'No,' the boy answered. 'Thanks.' He studied Carella again. 'Mind if I sit?'

'Public Park,' Carella said, shrugging.

The boy sat, his hands in his pockets. He watched Carella eating the peanuts. 'You come here to feed the pigeons or something?' he asked.

'Me?' Carella said.

'Yeah, you.'

Carella turned to face the boy fully. 'Who wants to know?' he asked.

'I'm just curious,' the boy said, shrugging.

'Listen,' Carella said, 'if you haven't got any business here near the lion house, go take a walk. You ask too many questions.'

The boy considered this for a long time. 'Why?' he said at last. 'You got business here?'

96

'My business is my business,' Carella said. 'Don't get snotty, kid, or you'll be picking up your teeth.'

'What're you getting sore about? I was only trying to find out . . .' He stopped abruptly.

'Don't try to find out anything, kid,' Carella said. 'You'll do better to keep your mouth shut. If you've got business here, just keep it to yourself, that's all. You never know who's listening.'

'Oh,' the kid said thoughtfully. 'Yeah, I hadn't thought of that.' He glanced over both shoulders, first peering to the left, then to the right. 'There's nobody around, though,' he said.

'That's true,' Carella answered.

'So, you know . . .' The boy hesitated again. Carella pretended to be interested in his peanuts. 'Listen, we're here for the same thing, ain't we?'

'Depends on what you're here for,' Carella said.

'Come on, mister, you know.'

'I'm here to get some air and eat some peanuts,' Carella said.

'Yeah, sure.'

'What are *you* here for?'

'You tell me first,' the boy said.

'You're new at this, ain't you?' Carella asked suddenly.

'Huh?'

'Look, kid, my advice to you is don't talk about the junk to anybody, not even me. How do you know I'm not a bull?'

'I never thought of that,' the boy said.

'Sure, you never thought of it. So if I was a bull, I could take you right in. Listen, when you've been on it as long as I have, you don't trust nobody.'

The boy grinned. 'So why you trusting me?' he asked.

' 'Cause I can see you're not a bull, and 'cause I can see you're new at the game.'

'I could be a bull,' the boy countered.

'You're too young. How old are you, eighteen?'

'I'm almost twenty.'

'So how could you be a bull?' Carella glanced at his watch. 'Dammit, what time was this meet supposed to be, anyway?'

'I was told four-thirty,' the boy said. 'You think anything happened to him?'

'Jesus, I sure hope not,' Carella said honestly. He was aware of a tense anticipation that began spreading through him. He had established now that there was to be a meet today, and that the meet was to have taken place at four-thirty. It was now almost five, which – barring any unforeseen accidents – meant that Gonzo should be showing any minute now.

'You know this Gonzo character?' the boy asked.

'Shhh, Jesus, don't use names,' Carella said, making a big show of looking around. 'Boy, you're real green.'

'Argh, nobody's here to listen,' the boy said cockily. 'Only a nut would be sitting out here in the cold. Unless he wanted to make a buy.'

'Or a pinch,' Carella said knowingly. 'Them damn cops can lay as still as a rock if they want to. You'd never know they was there until the cuffs are on your wrists.'

'There ain't no cops around. Listen, why don't you take a look for him?'

'This is my first time with him,' Carella said. 'I don't know what he looks like.'

'Neither do I,' the boy answered. 'Was you getting from Annabelle?'

'Yeah,' Carella said.

'Yeah, me too. He was a nice kid. For a spic.'

'Well, spics are okay,' Carella said, shrugging. He paused. 'You got no idea what this Gonzo looks like?'

'He's supposed to be a little bald. That's all I know.'

'He's an old man?'

'No, I don't think so. He's just a little bald. Lots of guys get a little bald, you know that, don't you?'

'Sure,' Carella said. He looked at his watch again. 'He should've showed by now, don't you think?'

'What time is it?'

'A little after five.'

'He'll be here.' The boy paused. 'How come this is your first time? I mean, with this Gonzo. Annabelle hung himself couple days back, didn't he?'

'Yeah, but I copped big from him before he pulled the plug. I had enough to tide me.'

'Oh,' the boy said. 'What I done, I've been shopping around, you know? I got some good stuff, but I also got a couple bum decks. I figure you got to do business with somebody you trust, don't you?'

'Sure, but how do you know you can trust this Gonzo?'

'I don't. What've I got to lose?'

'Well, hell, he may stick us with beat stuff.'

'I'm willing to chance it. Annabelle's stuff was always good.'

'Sure, it was. The best.'

'He was a good kid, Annabelle. For a spic.'

'Yeah,' Carella said.

'Don't get me wrong,' the boy said. 'I got nothing against spics.'

'Well, that's a good attitude,' Carella said. 'There are two things I can't stand, and that's bigots and spics.'

'Huh?' the boy said.

'Why don't you go take a walk and look for Gonzo? Maybe he's coming down the path.'

'I don't know him.'

'Neither do I. You check now, and if he ain't here in five minutes, I'll check next time.'

'Okay,' the boy said. He rose and walked away from the bench, toward where the path angled down sharply alongside one wall of the lion house.

The things that happened next happened with remarkable rapidity and in almost comic succession. Later, when Carella had a chance to think about the events clearly, unhampered by the subjective viewpoint of having been caught in them while they were happening, he was able to put them in their right sequence. As they happened, they only succeeded in annoying him and in stunning him somewhat. But later, he was able to see them clearly as a pattern of unfortunate coincidence.

He first watched the boy walk up to the path, stand there for a moment, and then shake his head at Carella, indicating that Gonzo was nowhere in sight. Then the boy turned and looked up the other end of the path and, perhaps so that he could get a better view, climbed to a small knoll and walked several paces until he was hidden by one corner of the lion house where the path swung around it. The instant the boy stepped out of sight, Carella was aware of someone approaching him from the opposite side of the lion house.

The someone approaching was a patrolman.

He walked briskly, and he wore ear muffs, and his face was very red, and he carried his night stick like a caveman's club. His direction was unmistakable. He was walking in a quick straight line that would take him directly to the bench upon which Carella was sitting. From the corner of his eye, Carella watched the turn in the path around which the boy had disappeared. The patrolman was closer now, walking purposefully and rapidly. He came up to the bench, stopped before Carella, and stared down at him. Carella glanced toward the path again. The boy had not yet returned into view.

'What're you doing?' the patrolman asked Carella.

Carella looked up. 'Me?' he said. He cursed the fact that the park was not part of his own precinct territory, cursed the fact that he did not know this patrolman, cursed the stupidity of the man, and at the same realized he could not show his credentials because the boy might return at any moment, and all he needed was for the boy to see him. And suppose Gonzo should arrive at this moment? Good God, suppose Gonzo should arrive?

'Yeah, you,' the patrolman said. 'There's only two of us here, ain't there?'

'I'm sitting,' Carella said.

'You been sitting for a long time now.'

'I like to sit in the fresh air,' Carella said, and he weighed the possibility of quickly flashing his shield, and the possibility of the patrolman quickly grasping the situation and taking off without another word. But as if to squash that possibility, the boy suddenly reappeared around the corner of the lion house, then stopped dead in his tracks, seeing the cop, and then reversed his field. But he did not disappear completely this time. This time he took up a post at the corner of the lion house, peering around the brick of the building like an advancing street soldier looking for possible snipers.

'Kind of cold to be sitting out here in the open, ain't it?' the patrolman asked. Carella looked up at him, and he could still see the boy watching behind the patrolman's back. There was

100

nothing he could do but try to talk himself out of this without revealing himself. That and pray that Gonzo would not arrive and be scared off by the sight of a uniform.

'Listen, is there any law against sitting on a bench and eating peanuts?' Carella asked.

'There might be.'

'Like what? I'm not bothering anybody, am I?'

'You might. You might try to molest the first young school-girl who walks by.'

'I'm not going to try to molest anybody,' Carella said. 'All I want to do is sit here and mind my own business and get some fresh air, that's all.'

'You could be a vagrant,' the patrolman said.

'Do I look like a vagrant?'

'Not exactly.'

'Look, officer . . .'

'You'd better stand up,' the patrolman said.

'Why?'

'Because I'll have to search you.'

'What the hell for?' Carella said angrily, constantly aware of the boy's prying eyes at the corner of the building, aware too that a search would uncover the .38 Detective's Special tucked in its holster into his waistband, and the gun would require an explanation, and the explanation would necessitate the flashing of tin, and there would go the set-up. The kid would know he was a cop, and the kid would take off, and if Gonzo showed at the same time . . .

'I got to search you,' the patrolman said. 'You may be a dope peddler or something.'

'Oh, for Christ's sake!' Carella exploded. 'Then go get a search warrant.'

'I don't need one,' the patrolman said calmly. 'You're either going to get searched or I'm going to clout you on the head and drag you into the station house as a vagrant. Now, how about it?'

The patrolman didn't wait for Carella's answer. He began running his night stick over Carella's body, and the first thing he hit was the .38. He yanked up Carella's jacket.

'Hey!' he shouted. 'What's this?'

His voice could easily have carried to the reptile house at the other end of the zoo. It certainly carried to the corner of the lion house not fifteen feet away, and Carella saw the boy's eyes open wide, and then the patrolman brandished the gun like a Carrie Nation hatchet, and the kid saw it, and his eyes narrowed suspiciously, and then his face vanished from the corner of the building.

'What is this?' the patrolman shouted again, holding Carella's arm now. Carella listened, and he heard footsteps beating a rapid retreat on the asphalt path. The boy was gone, and Gonzo hadn't shown either. In any case, the day was shot clear up the ass.

'I'm talking to you!' the patrolman shouted. 'You got a permit for this gun?'

'My name,' Carella said slowly and precisely, 'is Stephen Carella. I'm a 2nd Grade Detective, and I work out of the 87th Precinct, and you just prevented me from making a possible narcotics pinch.' The patrolman's red face turned a little pale. Carella looked at him sourly and said, 'Go ahead, panic. It'll serve you right.'

CHAPTER TWELVE

A FEATHER.

It was only a feather, but it was perhaps the most meaningful bit of evidence turned up in the room where Maria Hernandez had been stabbed.

There are all kinds of feathers.

There are chicken feathers, and duck feathers, and quail feathers, and goose feathers, and flamingo feathers, and horse feathers, and even Leonard Feathers.

Feathers are divided into two groups, down feathers and contour feathers.

The feather found in the room was a down feather.

Now, when a kid in the 87th Precinct held another kid in high regard, considered this kid an all-right guy, a courageous fighter, a lover, a hero, he might very well refer to the boy as a 'down cat'. The *cat* signifying *boy*, and the *down* signifying *all right*.

A down feather, on the other hand, was not an all-right feather. That is to say, there was nothing really wrong with it, but it was in no way courageous, amorous, brave, or trust-worthy. It simply happened to come from a certain part of a bird's body, as opposed to other parts of the body, and so it was called down rather than contour.

The down feather found in the room was allowed to soak in soapy water for a while, then rinsed under running water, and then rinsed again in alcohol, and then put under the micro-scope.

The feather had long knots consisting of several protruding tips.

In the order of sparrows, the knots are close together and conical.

In the order of wading birds, the knots are pointed and conical, the barbules hairy and hard.

Climbing birds have feathers with strongly protruding knots with four tips.

Aquatic birds have strong knots with dull points.

Chickens and other birds in the Gallinae order have feathers with the same characteristics as wading birds.

Pigeons . . . ah, pigeons.

Pigeon feathers have long knots consisting of several pro-truding tips.

The feather in the room was a pigeon feather.

The feathers in the one pillow on the bed were duck down. The feather found, therefore, had not come from the pillow. It was found stuck to a smear of blood, so chances were it was left by the killer and not left by someone who'd been in the room previous to the killer.

If the killer, therefore, had a pigeon feather stuck to his clothes, chances were he was a pigeon fancier.

All the cops had to do was track down every pigeon fancier in the city.

That job was for the birds.

The department stores on Friday, 22 December, were a little crowded. Bert Kling could not honestly say he disliked the crowds because the crowds forced him into close proximity with Claire Townsend, and there was no girl he'd rather have been proximately close to. On the other hand, however, the alleged purpose of this excursion was to pick up presents for people like Uncle Ed and Aunt Sarah – whom Kling had never met – and the sooner that task was accomplished, the sooner he and Claire could begin spending an uncluttered afternoon together. This was, after all, a day off and he did not enjoy trudging all over department stores on his day off, even if that trudging were being done with Claire.

He had to admit that of all the trudgers around, he and Claire made the nicest-looking pair of trudgers. There was a tireless sort of energy about her, an energy he usually associated with Phys Ed majors. Phys Ed majors were easily identified by short, squat bodies with muscular legs and bulging biceps. Claire Townsend had none of the attributes of the Phys Ed major, except the tireless energy.

Claire, in Kling's estimation, was perhaps the most beautiful woman alive. She was certainly the most beautiful woman he had ever met. Her hair was black. There are blacks, you know, and then there are blacks. But Claire's hair was a total black, a complete absence of light, a pure black. Her eyes were a warm brown, arched with black brows. She had the pale complexion of a high-bred Spanish girl coupled with the high cheek bones of an Indian. Her nose was straight and her mouth was full, and she was obviously the loveliest woman in the world. Whether she was or not doesn't matter. Kling thought she was.

He also thought she was a dynamo.

He wondered when the dynamo would run down, but the dynamo kept right on discharging electrical bolts and buying gifts for Cousin Percy and Grandmother Eloise, and Kling trailed along like a dinghy tied to a schooner in full sail, mixing his metaphors with reckless abandon.

'You should see what I got you,' she told him.

'What?' he asked.

'A gold-plated holster for your ridiculous weapon.'

'My gun, you mean?' he asked.

'And a carton of soap for your dirty mind.'

'I'll bet I could make 2nd Grade in ten minutes just picking up shoplifters here,' he said.

'Don't pick up any who are young or blonde.'

'Claire . . .'

'Look at those gloves! Only $2.98 and perfect for . . .'

'Cousin Antoinette in Kalamazoo. Claire . . .'

'As soon as I get these gloves, darling.'

'How do you know what I was going to say?'

'You want to stop all this nonsense and get some drinks, don't you?'

'Yes.'

'Just what I had in mind,' Claire said. And then, being in a gay and expansive mood, she added, 'You should be delighted. When we're married, *you'll* have to pay for all this junk.'

It was the first time the subject of marriage had come up between them and, being towed as he was, Kling almost missed it. Before he became fully aware of the miracle of what she had said, Claire had purchased the $2.98 gloves and was whisking him along to the roof garden of the store. The roof garden was packed with matronly women who were bulging with bundles.

'They only serve those triangular little sandwiches here,' Kling announced. 'Come on, I'll take you to a shady bar.'

The shady bar he took her to was really not quite so shady as all that. It was dim, true, but dimness and shadiness are not necessarily synonymous.

When the waiter tiptoed over, Kling ordered a Scotch on the rocks and then glanced inquisitively toward Claire.

'Cognac,' she said, and the waiter crept away.

'Are you really going to marry me some day?' Kling asked.

'Please,' Claire told him, 'I'll burst. I'm full of Christmas cheer, and a proposal now will just destroy me.'

'But you *do* love me?'

'Did I ever say so?'

'No.'

'Then what makes you so impetuous?'

'I'm sure you love me.'

'Well, confidence is a fine quality, to be sure, but . . .'

'Don't you?'

Claire sobered quite suddenly. 'Yes, Bert,' she said. 'Yes, Bert darling, I do love you. Very much.'

'Well then . . .' He was speechless. He grinned foolishly and covered her hand with his and blinked.

'Now I've spoiled you,' she said, smiling. 'Now that you know I'm in your power, you'll be unbearable.'

'No, no, I won't.'

'I know you policemen,' she insisted. 'You're brutal and cruel and . . .'

'No, Claire, no really, I . . .'

'Yes, yes. You'll take me in for questioning and . . .'

'Oh Jesus, Claire, I love you,' he said plaintively.

'Yes,' she said, smiling contentedly. 'Isn't it wonderful? Aren't we so lucky, Bert?'

'You were lucky,' the man said.

Gonzo looked at him sourly. 'Yeah? You think so?'

'You could have taken a fall. How much were you holding?'

'About an ounce. That's not the point. What I'm trying to tell you is that this is getting hot, you see?'

'We want it to get hot.'

'Listen, friend, hot is hot, but getting my own ass in a sling is another thing.'

'You weren't nabbed, were you?'

'No, but only because I happened to be on my toes.' Gonzo lighted a cigarette, and then exhaled a cloud of smoke. 'Listen, don't you understand what I'm saying?'

'I understand perfectly.'

'Okay, okay. This guy was a dick. And he was sure as hell looking for *me*! That means they're on to me some way, and that means they may know what happened in that room with Annabelle.'

'It doesn't matter what they know.'

'You keep saying that. Okay, play it cool. I'm saying we're in this pretty deep now, and I say let's get it over with. Make your goddamn call, do what has to be done. Get it over with.'

'I'll make the call when I'm ready,' the man said. 'I want to go up and look at the pigeons first. This cold weather . . .'

'You and your goddamn pigeons,' Gonzo said.

'Pigeons are good,' the man said simply.

'All right, look at them. Tuck them in. Do whatever you want. But call Byrnes, will you? Let's square this thing away. Remember, I got nothing to do with this but . . .'

'You've got a lot to do with it!'

'Nothing! That's what I'm trying to tell you. You made me a lot of promises, okay, I don't see nothing happening. All I see is bulls looking for me. Okay, what happened to the promises? What happened to your big idea? Goddammit, who was it told you Byrnes's kid was a junkie in the first place?'

'You, Gonzo.'

'Okay. So how about it? When do the promises pay off?'

'You've got Annabelle's trade, haven't you?'

'Peanuts!' Gonzo said vehemently. 'You laid this out like big time. Okay, where's the big time? Didn't I do everything you said? Didn't I risk my neck setting up the Hernandez girl? You think it was easy getting her to agree to lie?'

'Yes, I think it was easy. I think all you had to do was flash the twenty-five dollars.'

'Yeah, well, it wasn't all that easy. The guy was her brother, you know. And she sure as hell didn't figure he was getting measured for a coffin. Anyway, he was a nice kid. That part of the idea stunk.'

'It was the only way to do it.'

'You coulda done it plenty ways,' Gonzo said, 'but I don't even want to talk about it. I don't know nothing about murder, nothing. Annabelle and his sister are your headaches. That's another thing, you know? Why'd you hafta cut . . .?'

'Shut up!'

'Okay, okay. All I'm saying is this. That goddamn 87th is wise to something, and I got to protect myself. I ain't taking a fall for you or nobody else. If that dick starts giving me trouble – well, don't think I'm going along with him, friend. Nobody's going to work me over in no goddamn squad room.'

'What'll you do, Gonzo? If a cop tries to take you in?'

'I'll kill the son of a bitch,' Gonzo said.

'I thought you didn't know anything about murder.'

'I'm talking about these fancy wash jobs you figure out. I'm clear out of that mess, friend. All I want is what I was promised. For giving you the lead in the first place, and for setting up the Hernandez girl. Without me, you never woulda ...'

'You'll get everything you were promised. Do you know what's wrong with you, Gonzo?'

'No, tell me. I'm dying to hear what's wrong with me.'

'You still think small time. You're playing with something that's big time, and your mind is still laying on the garbage heap.'

'Well, your mind is up in the clouds. Congratulations. Excuse me for being in the garbage.'

'Start thinking big, you fool! Once I explain to Byrnes ...'

'When? Call him, will you? Let's get this thing rolling.'

'As soon as I check my pigeons.'

'Check on the pigeons!' Byrnes shouted into the intercom. 'If you've got stoolies, why the hell aren't you using them, Steve?'

At the other end of the instrument, Carella sighed patiently, unable to understand Byrnes's curious irritation these past few days.

'Pete, I *have* been checking with our stoolies. None of them seem to know anybody named Gonzo. I've got a call in right now to Danny Gimp. As soon as I ...'

'I find it impossible to believe that nobody in this goddamn precinct has ever head of Gonzo!' Byrnes shouted. 'I find it impossible to believe that with a squad of sixteen detectives, I can't locate a two-bit pusher when I want him! I'm sorry, Steve, but I find that pretty damn impossible to believe.'

'Well ...'

'Have you checked the other precincts? A man doesn't simply materialize out of thin air. That doesn't happen, Steve. If he's a pusher, he may have a record.'

'He may be a new pusher.'

'Then he may have a J.D. card.'

'No, I've checked that. Pete, maybe the Gonzo is a nickname. Maybe ...'

'What the hell do we have aliases files for?' Byrnes shouted.

'Pete, be reasonable. He may not be an old-timer. He may

be one of these young punks who's just cut himself into the business. So he has no record and he . . .'

'A young punk suddenly becomes a pusher, and you're telling me he has no J.D. record?'

'Pete, he doesn't necessarily have to be listed as a juvenile delinquent. It's just possible, you know, that he's never been in trouble. There are hundreds of kids in the streets who don't have cards on . . .'

'What are you telling me?' Byrnes said. 'Are you telling me you can't find a snotnosed punk for me, is that what? This Gonzo took over Hernandez's trade, and that's a possible motive for murder, don't you think?'

'Well, if it were a big enough trade, yes. But, Pete . . .'

'Have you got a better motive, Steve?'

'No, not yet.'

'Then find me Gonzo!'

'Ah, Jesus, Pete, you're talking to me as if . . .'

'I'm still running this squad, Carella,' Byrnes said angrily.

'All right, look. Look, I met a kid yesterday who was ready to make a buy from Gonzo. I know what the kid looks like, and I'll try to scout him up today, okay? But first let me see what Danny Gimp has.'

'You think this kid knows Gonzo?'

'He said he didn't yesterday, and he panicked when a patrolman showed. But maybe he's made contact since, and maybe he can lead me to Gonzo. I'll look around. Danny should be calling back in a half-hour or so.'

'All right,' Byrnes said.

'I don't know why you're getting so hot about this case,' Carella ventured. 'We're getting hardly any pressure at . . .'

'I get hot about *every* case,' Byrnes said tersely, and he snapped off the connexion.

He sat at his desk and stared through the corner window of the room, looking out over the park. He was very weary and very sad, and he hated himself for snapping at his men, and he hated himself for concealing important evidence, evidence that might possibly help a good cop like Carella. But again he asked himself the question, and again the question had the same hollow ring to it: *What's a man supposed to do?*

Would Carella understand? Or would Carella, being a good cop and a smart cop, beat those fingerprints to death, track them down, get to work in earnest and come up with a murderer named Larry Byrnes?

What am I afraid of? Byrnes asked himself.

And, faced with the answer, a new despondency claimed him. He knew what he was afraid of. He had met a new Larry Byrnes in the past few days. The new person masquerading as his son was not a very nice person. He did not know that person at all.

That person could have done murder.

My son, Larry, may have killed that Hernandez boy, Byrnes thought.

The phone on his desk rang. He listened to it ring for several moments, and then he swung his swivel chair around and picked up the receiver.

'87th Squad,' he said. 'Lieutenant Byrnes here.'

'Lieutenant, this is Cassidy at the desk.'

'What is it, Mike?'

'I've got a call for you.'

'Who is it?'

'Well, that's just it. The guy won't say.'

Byrnes felt a sudden sharp pain at the base of his spine. The pain spread, suffused slowly, became a warm dissipating glow. 'He . . . he wants to talk to me?' Byrnes asked.

'Yes, sir,' Cassidy said.

'All right, put him on.'

Byrnes waited. His hands were sweating. The receiver was slippery in his right hand, and he wiped the palm of his left hand on his trouser leg.

'Hello?' the voice said. It was the same voice as before. Byrnes recognized it instantly.

'This is Lieutenant Byrnes,' he said.

'Ah, good afternoon, Lieutenant,' the voice said. 'How are you?'

'I'm fine,' Byrnes said. 'Who is this?'

'Well now, that's not exactly a very bright question, is it, Lieutenant?'

'What do you want?'

'Ah, are we alone on this wire, Lieutenant? I'd hate to think that any of your colleagues were about to hear the personal things we'll discuss.'

'No one listens in on my calls,' Byrnes assured him.

'You're quite certain of that, are you, Lieutenant?'

'Don't take me for a fool,' Byrnes snapped. 'Say what you've got to say.'

'Have you had a chance to chat with your son, Lieutenant?'

'Yes,' Byrnes said. He shifted the phone to his left hand, wiped his right hand, and then switched again.

'And has he confirmed the accusations I made the last time I spoke to you?'

'He's a drug addict,' Byrnes said. 'That's true. . . .'

'A pity, isn't it, Lieutenant. Nice kid like that.' The voice grew suddenly businesslike. 'Did you check those fingerprints?'

'Yes.'

'Are they his?'

'Yes.'

'It looks bad, doesn't it, Lieutenant?'

'My son didn't argue with Hernandez.'

'I've got a witness, Lieutenant.'

'Who's your witness?'

'You'll be surprised.'

'Go ahead.'

'Maria Hernandez.'

'What!'

'Yes. That makes it look even worse, doesn't it? The one witness to the argument suddenly winds up dead. That makes it look pretty bad, Lieutenant.'

'My son was with me on the night Maria Hernandez was killed,' Byrnes said flatly.

'That'll sit pretty nicely with a jury, won't it?' the voice said. 'Especially when the jury learns Pop had been concealing evidence.' There was a pause. 'Or have you told your colleagues about your son's prints on that syringe?'

'No,' Byrnes said hesitantly. 'I . . . I haven't. Look, what is it you want?'

'I'll tell you what I want. You're supposed to be a pretty tough customer, aren't you, Lieutenant?'

'Goddammit, what do you want?' Byrnes paused. 'Are you looking for money? Is that it?'

'Lieutenant, you underestimate me. I . . .'

'Hello?' a new voice said.

'What?' Byrnes asked. 'Who . . .?'

'Oh, gee, I'm sorry, Lieutenant,' Cassidy said. 'I must've plugged into the wrong hole. I'm trying to get Carella. I've got Danny Gimp for him.'

'All right, Cassidy, get off the line,' Byrnes said.

'Yes, sir.'

He waited until the clicking told him Cassidy was gone.

'All right,' he said. 'He's gone.'

There was no answer.

'Hello?' Byrnes said. 'Hello?'

His party was gone. Byrnes slammed down the receiver, and then sat morosely at his desk, thinking. He thought very carefully, and he thought very clearly, and when the knock sounded on his door five minutes later, he had reached a conclusion and a certain peace.

'Come,' he said.

The door opened. Carella came into the office.

'I just spoke to Danny Gimp,' Carella said. He shook his head. 'No luck. He doesn't know any Gonzo, either.'

'Well,' Byrnes said wearily.

'So I'm going to take another run over to the park. Maybe I'll see this kid again. If he's not there, I'll try around.'

'Fine,' Byrnes said. 'Do your best.'

'Right.' Carella turned to leave.

'Steve,' Byrnes said, 'before you go . . .'

'Yes?'

'There's something you ought to know. There's a lot you ought to know.'

'What is it, Pete?'

'The fingerprints on that syringe –' Byrnes said, and then he girded himself for what would be a long and painful story. 'They're my son's.'

CHAPTER THIRTEEN

'MOM!'

Harriet stood at the foot of the steps and heard the voice of her son again, a plaintive voice that penetrated the wood of his door and then fled wildly down the steps.

'Mom, come up here! Open this door! Mom!'

She stood quite still, her eyes troubled, her hands clenched one over the other at her waist.

'*Mom!*'

'What is it, Larry?' she said.

'Come up here! Goddammit, can't you come up here?'

She nodded gently, knowing he could not see her reply, and she started up the steps to the upper level. She was a full-breasted woman who had been considered something of a beauty in her Calm's Point youth. Her eyes, even now, were a clear bright green, but the red of her hair was threaded with grey strands and she had put on more weight in the behind than she'd wanted. Her legs were still good, not as strong as they used to be, but good, clean legs. They carried her upstairs, and she stopped outside the door to Larry's bedroom and very quietly asked, 'What is it, son?'

'Open the door,' Larry said.

'Why?'

'I want to come out.'

'Your father said you are not to leave your room, Larry. The doctor ...'

'Oh, sure, Mom,' Larry said, his voice becoming suddenly oily, 'that was before. But I'm all right now, really I am. Come on, Mom, open the door.'

'No,' she said firmly.

'Mom,' Larry continued persuasively, 'can't you tell I'm all right now? Really, Mom, I wouldn't try to fool you. I'm fine. But I feel sort of cooped up here, really. I'd like to walk around the house a little, stretch my legs.'

'No.'

'Mom ...'

'No, Larry!'

'For Christ's sake, what the hell do I have to do around here, anyway? Are you trying to torture me? Is that what you're trying to do? Listen to me. Now listen to me, Mom. You go call that lousy doctor and tell him to get me something fast, do you hear?'

'Larry ...'

'Shut up! I'm sick of this damn mollycoddle attitude around here! All right, I'm a junkie! I'm a goddamn junkie, *and I want a fix!* Now, get it for me!'

'I'll call Johnny if you like. But he will not bring any heroin.'

'You're a pair, aren't you? You and the old man. Ike and Mike. They think alike. Open this door! *Open this goddamn door!* I'll jump out the window if you don't open it! You hear me? If you don't open this door, I'm gonna jump out the window.'

'All right, Larry,' Harriet said calmly. 'I'll open the door.'

'Oh,' he said. 'Well. It's about time. So open it.'

'Just a moment,' she said. She walked quite calmly and quite deliberately to her own bedroom at the end of the hall. She heard Larry call 'Mom!' but she didn't answer. She went directly to her dresser, opened the top drawer and took out a leather case. She snapped open the case, dust-covered because it had not been used since Peter gave it to her as a gift, and lifted the pearl-handled .22 from where it lay on its velvet bed. She checked the gun to make sure it was loaded, and then she walked down the corridor to Larry's door, the gun dangling loosely at her side.

'Mom?' Larry asked.

'Yes, just a moment.' She reached into the pocket of her apron for the key, inserting it into the lock with her left hand. She twisted the key, shoved open the door, levelled the .22, and stepped back.

Larry rushed for the door almost immediately. He saw the gun in his mother's hand, and then pulled up short, staring at her unbelievingly.

'Wh ... what's that?'

114

'Back away,' Harriet said, holding the gun quite steadily.

'Wh . . .'

She entered the room, and he moved away from her and the gun. She closed the door behind her, moved a straight-back chair to a position in front of the knob, and then sat in it.

'Wh . . . what's the gun for?' Larry asked. There was something in his mother's eyes that he could remember from his childhood days. It was something stern and reprimanding, something with which he could not argue. He knew. He had tried arguing with it when he was a little boy.

'You said you were going to jump out the window,' Harriet said. 'It's at least a forty-foot drop to the pavement, if not more. If you jump, Larry, you're liable to kill yourself. That's what the gun's for.'

'I . . . I don't understand.'

'This, son,' Harriet said. 'You're not leaving this room, either by the door *or* the window. And if you make a move toward either of them, I'll have to shoot you.'

'What!' Larry said incredulously.

'Yes, Larry,' Harriet said. 'I'm a good shot, too. Your father taught me, and he was the best damn shot at the academy. Now sit down and let's talk, shall we?'

'You're . . .' Larry swallowed. 'You're k . . . kidding me, of course.'

'It would,' Harriet answered, 'be a little foolish to gamble on that premise, son, considering the fact that it's me who's holding the gun.'

Larry looked at the .22 and then blinked.

'Now sit,' Harriet said, smiling pleasantly, 'and we'll talk about all sorts of things. Have you thought of what you're giving Dad for Christmas?'

There's a trouble with murder.

There are, to be truthful, a lot of troubles with murder – but there's one in particular.

It gets to be a habit.

No one's claiming, you understand, that murder is the only habit-forming activity around. That would be untrue and somewhat foolish. Brushing the teeth is habit forming. So is taking

115

a bath. So is infidelity. So is going to the movies. Living, if one wanted to be a little morbid, is also a little habit forming.

But murder is, and in a non-exclusive way, definitely habit forming.

That's the main trouble with murder.

The man who killed Aníbal Hernandez had a very good reason, according to his own somewhat curious way of thinking, for wanting Aníbal dead. Now, if you're going to justify murder at all, you'd have to admit that so far as good reasons went, this fellow had a pretty good one. All within the framework of murder, of course. There are good reasons and bad reasons for everything, and there are doubtless many people who might feel that there simply is no such thing as a good reason for murder. Well, there's no arguing with some diehards.

But this fellow's reason was a good one, and once the somewhat gory task of murder had been done, the reason seemed even better because a *fait accompli* seeks and generally finds its own justification.

The reason for killing Aníbal's sister also seemed to be a pretty good one at the time. Hadn't the fool girl exhibited all the symptoms of a tongue about to start wagging? Besides, a girl shouldn't start arguing with a man when he ... well, it served her right. Of course, she really hadn't known anything, except about Gonzo, well, that was reason enough. Tell the police that Gonzo had asked her to lie, and then the police would pick up Gonzo, and Gonzo would empty his stomach of everything. That was dangerous.

Standing now in his pigeon coop on the roof, he could see how dangerous it would be if Gonzo got picked up. He was still a little rattled by the fact that Byrnes had put a tap on their call, even though he'd been assured no one was listening. That would seem to indicate a foolhardiness on the part of Byrnes, and one doesn't get very foolhardy when his son might be involved, unless one has an ace up his sleeve. And what could that ace be?

God, it was windy up here on the roof. He was glad he had put tar paper over the wire mesh of the coop. Sure, pigeons are hardy, don't they go gallivanting around Grover Park all winter long, but still he wouldn't want any of his birds to die. There was one in particular, that little female fantail, who didn't look good at all. She had not eaten for several days now and her eyes, if you could tell anything at all from a pigeon's eyes, didn't look right. He would have to watch her, maybe get something into her with an eye-dropper. The other birds were looking fine, though. He had several Jacobins, and he would never tire of watching them, never tire of admiring the hoodlike ruff of feathers they wore around their heads. And his tumbler, God, the way that bird somersaulted when it flew, or how about the pouters, they were magnificent birds, too, what the hell could Byrnes have up his sleeve?

How had a dick got on to Gonzo's tail?

Was it possible the girl had talked? Before she'd died? No, that was not possible. If she had talked, the police would have come to him directly and damn fast. They wouldn't be fooling around trying to pick up Gonzo. Then how? Had someone seen Gonzo talking to her on the afternoon of Annabelle's death? That was possible, yes.

How had this thing got so complicated?

It had started as a simple plan, and now the plan didn't seem to be working, should he call Byrnes again, tell Byrnes there had better not be anyone listening this time, tell him the whole damned story, lay the cards right on the table? But who could have seen the girl with Gonzo? Had they talked together in the same room she'd taken him to? The room Maria got from that woman, what was her name? Dolores? Wasn't that what she'd said? Yes, Dolores. Had Dolores known about Gonzo's talk with Maria? Had she recognized Gonzo from seeing him before, not knowing his name perhaps but . . . no. No, the police were probably keeping all known pushers under surveillance. But Gonzo is *not* a known pusher.

Gonzo is a punk who happened to stumble across some valuable information and who fortunately placed that information in the hands of someone who realized its potential: me.

Gonzo has no record, Gonzo is not a known pusher, Gonzo is in this only for the promise of quick unhindered riches, and he is not even known in the neighbourhood, not as Gonzo, anyway. So if he has no record, and if he is not known as

Gonzo, and if he is not a known pusher, how did the police find out about him?

The woman.

Dolores.

No, not her, but someone perhaps saw them talking together that afternoon, saw him extract from her the promise of a lie, saw the twenty-five dollars exchange hands. Someone perhaps...

How much did Maria tell the woman Dolores?

Good Christ, why am I worrying about Gonzo? How much did Maria tell that old woman? Did she mention my name to her? Did she say, 'I have this friend who wants to sleep with me, and I need a room?' Did she then say who the friend was, God, could she have been so stupid?

What does Dolores know?

He took a last look at the female fantail, stepped out of the coop, locked the door, and then went downstairs to the street. He walked with a brisk spring in his step. He walked with a purpose and a goal, and that goal was the tenement building in which he and Maria had shared a room. When he reached the building, he looked both ways up the street, thankful the streets were not crowded, thankful for winter because if this were summer, the front stoop would be crowded with old women yacketing.

He checked the mailboxes, finding one marked DOLORES FAURED. Yes, that was the name Maria had mentioned. Dolores Faured. The apartment was on the second floor. He walked through the hallway quickly. There was no pain of remembrance in his mind. What had happened with Maria Hernandez had happened, and murder is habit forming.

He found the apartment and knocked.

'Quién es?' a voice called.

'Un amigo,' he answered, and he waited.

He heard footsteps, and then the door opened. The woman standing there was thin and frail, a frail old witch, he could pick her up and break her in half if he wanted to. With sudden insight, he realized that he was now committed. He had come here, and if the old woman knew nothing, if Maria had indeed

118

told her nothing, what then? How did he question her and still leave her with no knowledge?

'Who are you?' the woman asked.

'May I come in?'

'What do you want?'

She would not let him into the house until she knew who he was, that was certain. But if he mentioned the name of Maria Hernandez, would he not then be tied to this frail old hag? Would she not then have a glimmer of knowledge? And was not even a glimmer of knowledge dangerous, how had this thing got so complicated?

'I'm from the police,' he lied. 'I want to ask some questions.'

'Come in, come in,' Dolores said. 'More questions, always questions.'

He followed her into the apartment. It was a dirty, smelly apartment, this woman was nothing but a female pimp, a frail witch of a pimp.

'What now?' she asked.

'On the night Miss Hernandez was killed? Did she mention to you who she was seeing? Who the man was?'

Dolores was staring at him. 'Don't I know you?' she asked.

'Not unless you've been inside the 87th Precinct,' he answered quickly.

'Haven't I seen you in the neighbourhood?'

'Well, I work in the neighbourhood. Naturally . . .'

'I thought I knew all the bulls from the 87th,' Dolores said speculatively. 'Well.' She shrugged.

'About this man.'

'*Sí.* Don't you cops work together?'

'What?'

'I already told them this. The others who came. Detectives Meyer and . . . who was the other?'

'I don't remember.'

'Hengel,' Dolores said. 'Yes, Detective Hengel.'

'Of course,' he said. 'Yes. Hengel. You already told them this?'

'Certainly. The next day. That room downstairs was flooded with police. Meyer and . . .' She stopped suddenly. 'It was

Temple,' she said, her eyes narrowing. 'Temple was the other cop's name.'

'Yes,' he said. 'What did you tell them?'

'You said Hengel.'

'What?'

'Hengel. You said it was Hengel.'

'No,' he said, 'you're mistaken. I said Temple.'

'I said Hengel, and you said yes, it was Hengel,' Dolores insisted.

'Well, we have a Hengel at the station house, too,' he said irritably. 'In any case, what did you tell them?'

Dolores looked at him long and hard. Then she said, 'Let me see your badge.'

Well, here we are doing the lion house bit again, Carella thought.

This is Steve Carella, folks, coming to you again from atop lovely Hotel Grover in the charming Lion House room. Ah, I hear the orchestra tuning up, ladies and gentlemen, so perhaps we'll have some delightful cocktail music. We broadcast from this spot every day at the same time, you know, through the auspices of the National Foundation for Contracting Double Pneumonia. We get a lovely little breeze here atop the Hotel Grover, and the breeze is never quite so charming as when it whips around the corners of the Lion House room. So stay tuned, folks, for a lot of laughs and a few surprises.

The surprises today include an announcement from Detective-Lieutenant Peter Byrnes, my immediate superior, who wishes you to know that his son Larry Byrnes was today voted Drug Addict of the Year cum Murder Suspect. Now, how's that for a little surprise, folks? Knock the wind out of you? Damn near knocked me flat on my ass, so the least it should do is knock a little wind out of you. What's that? Excuse me, folks, I'm being signalled from Hy Auerglass in the control booth. What is it, Hy? Oh, we've been cut off the air? That last 'ass' did it, huh? Well, those are the breaks. I can always go back to being a cop.

Oh, that poor son of a bitch. I like that guy. There are cops who don't like him, but I do, and I wouldn't have another

120

skipper if he came gold-plated. But what's he going through right now? What's he going through, with some bastard sitting out there and dangling a carrot in front of his nose, what's he . . .

He spotted the boy.

The same boy he'd talked to yesterday afternoon, only the boy wasn't heading for the lion house this time. Was it possible that run-in with the patrolman yesterday had scared Gonzo into calling the meet for elsewhere in the park?

The boy had not seen him, and chances were he would not recognize him even if he did see him. Carella was wearing a battered felt hat with the rim rolled down front, sides, and back. He wore a wide box raincoat which gave him an appearance of girth. And, even though it made him feel a little silly, he was wearing a false moustache. The raincoat was buttoned from top to bottom; Carella's .38 was in the right-hand pocket.

Quickly, he took off after the boy.

The boy seemed to be in a hurry. He walked straight past the lion house, up the knoll in the path, and then hesitated at a sign which read – pointing in several directions – Seals, Reptiles, Children's Zoo. The boy nodded, and then began walking in the direction of the reptiles.

Carella thought of overtaking the boy and asking him some pointed questions. But if the boy were rushing to meet Gonzo, wouldn't it be a little ridiculous to stop him? The object all sublime was to net a pusher who may have had something to do with the demise of Aníbal Hernandez. Junkies making buys could be had by the basketful. Gonzo was the important character in this business transaction, and so Carella bided his time, following the blond boy and waiting for the big deal the way a stockbroker waits for a merger between Ford and Chrysler.

The boy seemed in no particular hurry. He seemed intent, instead, on making a thorough inspection of what the zoo offered. Wherever there was an animal, the boy stopped to look at it. Occasionally, he glanced over his shoulder. Once he stopped to consult a big clock set in the face of the monkeys', apes', and gorillas' house. He nodded and then moved on.

Apparently, there was still time. Apparently, the meet had been called for – what time was it now? Carella looked at his watch. It was three-fifteen. Was three-thirty a safe estimate? Was that why his young friend was dawdling all over the park?

The dawdling eventually took the blond boy to the men's room. He walked up the flag-covered path, and Carella watched him. As soon as the boy entered the building, Carella circled it, checking for a second exit door. There was none. Satisfied that the boy could not leave the building in any way but through the door by which he had entered, Carella sat on a bench and prepared to wait out the vagaries of nature.

He waited for five minutes. At the end of that time, the boy reappeared and began travelling at a fast trot in the direction of the reptile house. Whatever other faults there may have been in the boy's judgement, Carella could not venture to guess. But he had certainly been astute in choosing the snake pit as an appropriate spot to meet a pusher. Carella grinned and followed toward the snakes, a sudden gay mood overtaking him. He was looking forward to the pinch, the way a good coon dog looks forward to the moment of the kill, just before the wounded coon drops out of the tree.

As if to add to his sudden happy outlook, a crowd magically appeared. It was as if a movie director cued his musicians for a crescendo, and then signalled for throngs to swarm out of the hills, building to a climactic scene.

The people who suddenly appeared were not exactly what Carella would have called throngs. They were, instead, the students of a junior high school class, led by a slightly embarrassed-looking male teacher whose principal had undoubtedly decided his charges were not getting enough 'real' experience. The principal had decided to introduce them to 'life', and so the science teacher had probably been asked to take his class to the zoo, where they could smell the animals. The teacher's face bore the expression of a man sitting next to two drunks in a subway; his mouth yearned to shout, 'They're not with me!'

But, unfortunately, the kids were with him, and they were the noisiest damn kids Carella had ever seen or heard. He did not mind the noise because there was a noise within him now, an excitement that mounted as he followed his prey past the school kids and hurried down the path toward the reptile house.

Behind him, one of the kids was saying, 'They got a snake in there can eat a pig whole, how about that?'

Another kid answered, 'There ain't no snakes can eat pigs whole.'

'No? That's how much you know. My father saw a Frank Buck pitcher where the snake eats a pig whole. And they got that snake here.'

'The *same* snake?'

'Not the one in the pitcher, stupid. But a snake like him.'

'Then how do you know this one can eat pigs?'

Fascinated as Carella was, he concentrated on his quarry. His quarry was entering the house with the snakes, and Carella did not want to lose him. For a ridiculous moment, he had the sneaking suspicion his moustache was falling off. He stopped, touched the area beneath his nose, and then, satisfied, entered the building. The boy seemed to know exactly where he was going. He didn't look at any of the snakes he passed, even though the zoo officials had gone to considerable expense in capturing, transporting, and suitably enclosing the reptiles. He walked directly to a cage behind whose thick plate-glass window lay two cobras. He stood watching the cobras, fascinated – or at least seemingly fascinated. Once or twice he rapped on the glass.

Carella took up a station alongside a small glass-fronted cage that contained a Rocky Mountain rattler. The snake was asleep, or dead, or some damn thing. It lay in a despondent coil, looking for all the world as if an earthquake would not have disturbed it. But Carella was not interested in the snake. Carella was interested in the colour of the glass cage that held the snake. For the back wall of that cage was painted a deep green, and from where Carella was standing, the plate-glass front combined with the green back wall to provide an excellent mirror effect. He could, while ostensibly marvelling over the rattle on the surely dead snake in the cage, study the boy across the room with considerable ease.

The boy was undoubtedly a snake lover. He was making sounds at the cobra cage, and he was rapping on the plate-glass front again, and he looked something like a new father in a hospital nursery, making an ass of himself through the nursery window.

The boy did not make an ass of himself for long, nor was he alone for very much longer. Carella couldn't hear any of the sounds emanating from the vicinity of the cobra cage because the junior high school class suddenly burst into the reptile house *en masse*, and the resultant chaos was a tribute to the city's school system. But Carella's quarry was no longer rapping on the glass. A second boy had come up to the cobra cage, a boy with a mane of wild black hair, wearing a black leather jacket, wearing black pegged trousers and black shoes.

Carella took one look at the newcomer and instantly thought: Gonzo.

Gonzo or not, the newcomer was the person Carella's young friend had been waiting for. Still unable to hear anything because of the science class, Carella was nonetheless able to witness a quick shaking of hands. Then both boys reached into their pockets simultaneously, and then there was another shaking of hands, and Carella knew the junk and the money for the junk had been exchanged.

Carella was no longer interested in his young friend. He was now interested in the boy with the black leather jacket. The blond boy he'd been following grinned, turned, and headed off in one direction. Carella let him go. The other boy lifted the collar of his black jacket, hesitated just a moment, and then headed off in the opposite direction. It was Carella's devout wish to collar him with a pile of narcotics on his person. It was also his desire to get him in the Squad Room and question him about the late Aníbal Hernandez.

Unfortunately, the school system was working against Carella that day.

He had shoved himself away from the front of the rattler cage and was taking off after the black leather jacket when a blood-curdling shriek split the air.

'There he is!' an adolescent voice screeched.

The screech, had it come from behind a tree in the heart of the jungle, would have been enough to send the brave hunter

124

scurrying for the nearest trading depot. As it was, it almost lifted the false moustache from Carella's upper lip.

In a moment, he realized what all the commotion was about. The kid had spotted the python cage, and was rushing over to it to see if any pigs were being devoured whole that afternoon. In another moment, Carella realized that he was in the direct path of a headlong stampede, and – unless he sidestepped damned fast – he might very well be devoured whole himself. He sidestepped damned fast, and the thundering herd rushed past him, and trailing in its wake came the weary and abashed shepherd, still wearing his 'They're not with me!' look.

The shouts and cries from the python cage were almost inhuman. Carella turned. The black leather jacket was gone.

He rushed to the door, cursing principals and science classes and Frank Buck, coming out into the cold air, feeling the bite of it on his cheeks, feeling it attack his teeth. The black leather jacket was nowhere in sight.

He began running, running aimless actually, not knowing which side of the path the boy had chosen. He kept running until it became obvious he had lost the boy. He was ready to start cursing all over again when he spotted the blond boy he'd been following earlier.

The blond boy was certainly not the one he wanted, but any port in a storm. The kid had just made a buy from Gonzo, hadn't he? All right, he'd found out about the meet someplace, and maybe he knew where Gonzo could be located. In any case, there was no time to lose. What with the city system rampaging all over the town, one never knew when one might run into a kindergarten class out hunting snipes. Carella moved fast.

He came up behind the boy almost soundlessly, and then he moved alongside him, and reached for his sleeve.

'All right . . .' he started, and the boy turned.

For a moment, the boy's face was blank. And then his eyes penetrated the false moustache, widened in recognition, and then turned alert with the knowledge of imminent danger. He shoved out at Carella instantly, surprising him, knocking him backward several paces.

'Hey!' Carella shouted, and the boy was off.

The boy may not have been a track star, but he certainly could run like a bastard.

Before Carella caught his breath, the kid was turning the bend of the path and heading into the trees. Carella started after him. He couldn't understand why the kid was risking more trouble than a small narcotics buy was worth, but he didn't stop to question motive too long. There was a time for thinking and theorizing, and a time for doing; and this was definitely a time for using legs and not brains. It was also a time for using firearms, but Carella wasn't aware of this as yet, and so the .38 stayed where it was in his right-hand coat pocket. There certainly didn't seem to be any danger attached to the simple task of overtaking and putting a collar on a junkie. Sublimely unaware of what was in store for him, Carella began climbing off the side of the path and into the trees.

He saw the blond head duck behind a boulder. He quickened his pace, panting hard, reflecting that he was not as young as he used to be. He was deep in the trees now, climbing over big boulders and smaller rocks, far from the path that wound through the park. He could see the blond head bobbing along in the distance, and then he didn't see it again, and he was afraid he'd lost *this* boy, too. He swung around a huge outcropping of rock, and then pulled up short.

He was looking into the open end of a .32.

'Don't open your mouth, cop,' the boy said.

Carella blinked. He had not expected a gun, and he cursed his own stupidity, and at the same time he sought for a way out of this. He looked at the kid's eyes, and the kid didn't seem to be high, so perhaps he could be talked to, perhaps reason could penetrate. But the .32 was held in a steady fist, and the eyes above the gun were unreasonable eyes.

'Listen . . .' he started.

'I said keep the mouth closed. I'll shoot you, cop.' The boy delivered the speech so simply that all of its lethalness seemed innocuous. But there was nothing innocuous about the boy's eyes, and Carella watched those eyes carefully. He had been on the business end of a gun before, and it was his contention that a man always telegraphed the tightening of his trigger finger by a previous tightening of his eyes.

'Keep your hands away from your sides,' the boy said. 'Where is it?'

'Where's what?'

'The gun that patrolman turned up yesterday. Still got it in your waistband?'

'How do you know I'm a cop?' Carella asked.

'The holster. Don't ask me about intuition. None of the guys I know who carry pieces carry them in holsters. Fish it out for me, cop.'

Carella's hand moved.

'No!' the boy said. 'Tell me where it is. I'll get it myself.'

'Why are you buying yourself trouble, kid? You could have got out of this with a simple misdemeanour.'

'Yeah?'

'Sure. Put the gun up. I'll forget you ever had it.'

'What's the matter, cop? You scared?'

'Why should I be scared?' Carella asked, watching the boy's eyes. 'I don't think you'd be silly enough to shoot me here in the park.'

'No, huh? You got any idea how many people are shot in this park every day?'

'How many, son?' Carella asked, stalling for time, wondering how he could get the .38 out of his pocket, divert the kid for an instant while he drew and fired.

'Plenty. Why are you following me, cop?'

'You won't believe this . . .' Carella started.

'Then don't waste it. Give me the real story the first time around.'

'I was after your pal.'

'Yeah? Which pal? I got lots of pals.'

'The one you met by the cobra cage.'

'Why him?'

'I've got some questions to ask him.'

'About what?'

'That's my business.'

'Where's your piece, cop? Tell me that first.'

Carella hesitated. He saw the boy's eyes tighten almost imperceptibly. 'My right-hand coat pocket,' he said quickly.

'Turn around,' the boy said.

Carella turned.

'Put the hands up. Don't try any tricks, cop, I'm warning you. You feel this? It's the muzzle of this piece. It'll be right up against your spine all the while I'm reaching into your pocket. You start to turn, you start to run, you even start to breathe crooked, and you've got a broken spinal cord. I ain't afraid to pull this trigger, so don't test me. You got that?'

'I've got it,' Carella said.

He felt the boy's hand move quickly into his pocket. In an instant, the reassuring weight of the .38 was gone.

'All right,' the boy said, 'turn around again.'

Carella turned to face him. He had not, up to that moment, really believed the situation to be a serious one. He had talked himself out of similar situations before, and he had been fairly certain – up to now – that he could either talk his way out of this one, or somehow get to the gun in his coat pocket. But the gun was no longer in his coat pocket, and the boy's eyes were hard and bright, and he had the peculiar feeling that he was staring sudden death in the face.

'You'd be stupid,' he heard himself say, but the words sounded hollow and insincere. 'You'd be shooting me for no reason. I told you I'm not after you.'

'Then why were you asking me all those questions yesterday? You thought you were playing it real cool, didn't you, cop? Sounding me out about the meet. I was sounding you at the same time. It ain't easy, you know, not when you don't know what faces are gonna be at a meet. It ain't easy at all. I let you think I was stepping right into your pitches, but I saw your curves coming a mile off. That patrolman clinched it for me. When he dug that piece out of your pants, I knew for sure you were a bull. Up to then, I could only smell it on you.'

'I'm still not after you,' Carella said patiently. They were standing on loose rock in the shadow of the big boulder. Carella weighed the possibility of lunging at the boy suddenly, throwing him off balance on the loose rock, getting the gun away from him. The possibility seemed extremely remote.

'No, huh? Look, cop, don't snow me. I've been snowed by the best. You think you're going to tie me in to something big, don't you? You think you're gonna get me in your cosy little precinct house and beat the crap out of me until I'll confess to having raped my own mother. Well, you're wrong, cop.'

'Goddammit, what do I want with a two-bit junkie?' Carella said.

'Me? A junkie? Come off it, will you? This time I'm not taking the pitches, cop. Don't try to sell me a new line of spitballs.'

'What's with you, anyway?' Carella asked. 'I've seen junkies panic before, but you're the uneasiest. Are you so scared of taking a fall? Dammit, I was only going to ask some questions about the guy you met. Can't you get that through your head? I don't want you. I want him.'

'I thought you weren't interested in two-bit junkies,' the boy said.

'I'm not.'

'Then why bother with him? He's eighteen years old, and he's been hooked since he was fourteen. He goes to bed with H. You're inconsistent, cop.'

'He's a pusher, isn't he?' Carella asked, puzzled.

'Him?' The boy began laughing. 'Cop, you're a riot.'

'What's...'

'All right, listen to me,' the boy said. 'You were tailing me yesterday, and you were tailing me today. I'm carrying enough junk on me right now to make a pinch pretty much worth your while. I'm also violating the Sullivan Act because I ain't got a licence for this piece. You've got me on resisting an officer, and there's probably some kind of law against taking a cop's gun from him, too. You got me, cop. You can throw the book at me. And if I cut out now, you'll grab me tomorrow, and then it's your word against mine.'

'Listen, take off. Put up the gun and take off,' Carella said. 'I'm not looking for a slug, and I'm not looking for trouble with you. I told you once. I want your pal.' Carella paused. 'I want Gonzo.'

'I know,' the boy said, his eyes tightening. '*I'm Gonzo.*'

The only warning was the tightening of Gonzo's eyes. Carella saw them squinch up, and he tried to move sideways, but the gun was already speaking. He did not see it buck in the boy's fist. He felt searing pain lash at his chest, and he heard the shocking declaration of three explosions and then he was falling, and he felt very warm, and he also felt very ridiculous because his legs simply would not hold him up, how silly, how very silly, and his chest was on fire, and the sky was tilting to meet the earth, and then his face struck the ground. He did not put out his arms to stop his fall because his arms were somehow powerless. His face struck the loose stones, and his body crumpled behind it, and he shuddered and felt a warm stickiness beneath him, and only then did he try to move and then he realized he was lying in a spreading pool of his own blood. He wanted to laugh and he wanted to cry at the same time. He opened his mouth, but no sound came from it. And then the waves of blackness came at him, and he fought to keep them away, unaware that Gonzo was running off through the trees, aware only of the engulfing blackness, and suddenly sure that he was about to die.

It is to the credit of the 87th that it worked faster than either of the two precincts that reigned over Grover Park. Carella was not found by a patrolman until almost a half-hour later, at which time the blood around him resembled a small swimming pool.

But another act of violence had been done in the 87th at about the same time Carella was being shot outside his precinct, and the results of that violence were discovered not ten minutes later.

The patrolman who called it in said, 'She's an old woman. Her neighbours tell me her name is Dolores Faured.'

'What's the story?' the desk sergeant asked.

The patrolman said, 'Her neck is broken. She either fell or was pushed down an airshaft from the second floor.'

CHAPTER FOURTEEN

IN the heart of the city, the shoppers went about their business. The store fronts glowed like hot pot-belly stoves, inviting the cold citizens to come in and toast awhile, come in and browse awhile, come in and buy a little. The swank shops lining plush Hall Avenue were decked not in holly but in an austerely shrieking display of Christmas white and red and green electrical wizardry. The front of one department store was covered with a two-storey-high display of blue angels, and the outdoor gardens across the street picked up the theme, multiplied it by a hundred, splashed the concrete with ethereal winged messengers of the Lord, escorting the passers-by to the giant Christmas tree near the skating rink. The tree climbed to the sky, ablaze with red and blue and yellow globes as big as a man's head, competing with the stiff formality of the giant office buildings around it.

The other shops dripped with incandescence, molten Christmas trees fashioned of light, giant white wreaths, windows aglow with the pristine brilliance of a new snowfall. The shoppers hurried in the streets, their arms loaded with packages. The office parties were in full swing behind the stiff formal fronts of the buildings. File clerks kissed file clerks behind banks of file cabinets. Bosses lifted the skirts of secretaries, and promotions were promised, and raises were bandied about like memo slips, and boys from the shipping departments tilted glasses with executives from wood-panelled offices. There were lipstick stains, and Scotch stains, and hurried phone calls to waiting wives, and hurried phone calls to husbands who were enjoying their own Christmas parties behind the equally stiff fronts of other buildings. There was happiness of a sort because this was late Friday afternoon, 22 December, and this was the culmination of a long year's waiting. And the accountant who'd had his discreet marital eye on the pretty, young, blonde receptionist could now greet her with more than a polite 'Good morning'. Sharing a highball by the water cooler, his arm could encircle her waist in Christmas friendliness. Her head could rest upon his shoulder in yuletide camaraderie. He could take her lips beneath the mistletoe, and he could do all this without the slightest feeling of guilt because the Christmas Party was an established tradition of the American culture. Husbands went to Christmas parties, and wives were never invited. Wives did not expect to be invited. For one day a year, the marital contract was temporarily revoked. Christmas parties were joked about later, the way a person will joke about a bloody dagger on his living-room coffee table, unwilling to acknowledge how it got there.

And in the streets, the shoppers walked. Time was short, and time was running out. The advertising executives who had goaded the public since before Thanksgiving were now busy getting drunk in their offices. But the public, caught in the commercial machinations of a holiday that had somehow grown out of all proportion to the simple birth in Bethlehem it represented, hurried and scurried and wondered and worried. Had Josephine's gift been expensive enough? Were all the Christmas cards mailed? What about the tree, shouldn't the tree have been bought by now?

Beneath it all, despite the gaudy plot of the advertising master minds, despite the frantic commercial rat race it had become, there was something else. There was, for some of the people, a feeling they could not have described if they'd wanted to. This was Christmas. This was the holiday season. Some of the people saw through the sham and the electrical glitter and the skinny Santa Clauses with straggly beards lining Hall Avenue. Some of the people felt something other than what the advertising men wanted them to feel. Some of the people felt good, and kind, and happy to be alive. Christmas did that to some people.

And so the city was drunken, and the city was goaded into near panic, and the streets were jammed with shoppers, and maybe the concrete looked cold and stiff and aloof – but it was the most wonderful city in the world, and it was never more wonderful than at Christmastime.

'This is Danny Gimp,' the man told the desk sergeant. 'I want to speak to Detective Carella.'

The desk sergeant didn't enjoy talking to stool pigeons. He knew that Danny Gimp often came up with good information, but he considered all stool pigeons unclean, and it was an offence just talking to them.

'Detective Carella isn't here,' the desk sergeant said.

'Do you know where I can reach him?' Danny asked. Danny was a man who'd been stooling for the police for as long as he could remember. He knew he was not respected for his talkative traits among members of the underworld, but the ensuing ostracism did not disturb him. Danny made his living as an informer and, quite curiously, he enjoyed helping the police. He had had polio as a child, with the result that one leg still carried a slight limp. His real surname was Nelson but very few people knew that, and even his mail came addressed to Danny Gimp. He was fifty-four years old, and very small all over, looking more like an undernourished adolescent than a full-grown man. His voice was high and reedy, and his face bore hardly any of the wrinkles or other telltale signs of age. He could not honestly say he liked cops, even though he liked helping them. There was one cop he did like. That cop was Steve Carella.

'Why do you want to reach him?' the desk sergeant asked.

'I think I may have some dope for him.'

'What kind of dope?'

'When did you get promoted to the detective division?' Danny asked.

'If you want to get smart, stoolie, you can get off the line.'

'I want Carella,' Danny said. 'Will you tell him I called?'

'Carella ain't taking any messages,' the desk sergeant said.

'What do you mean?'

'He got shot this afternoon. He's dying.'

'What!'

'You heard me.'

'What!' Danny said again, stunned. 'Steve got ... Are you kidding me?'

'I'm not kidding you.'

'Who shot him?'

'That's what we'd like to know.'

'Where is he?'

'General Hospital. Don't bother going down. He's on the critical list, and I doubt if they're letting him talk to stoolies.'

'He's not really dying,' Danny said, almost as if to reassure himself. 'Listen, he's not really dying, is he?'

'They found him half-froze and almost bloodless. They've been pumping plasma into him, but he took three slugs in the chest, and it don't look good.'

'Ah, listen,' Danny said. 'Ah, Jesus.' He was silent for a while.

'You finished, stoolie?'

'No, I . . . General Hospital, did you say?'

'Yeah. I told you, stoolie, don't bother going down. It'd make you uncomfortable. Half the bulls on the squad are there.'

'Yeah,' Danny said thoughtfuly. 'Jesus, that's a tough break, ain't it?'

'He's a good cop,' the desk sergeant said simply.

'Yeah,' Danny said. He was silent again, and then he said, 'Well, so long.'

'So long,' the desk sergeant said.

Because of the sergeant's warning, Danny Gimp did not get to the hospital until the next morning. He wrestled with the problem all that Friday night, wondering if his presence would be welcome, wondering if Carella would even recognize him. And even if Carella was in condition to say hello, Danny doubted if he'd want to. They had a going business arrangement, but Danny was keenly aware of the fact that an informer is not the most respected of men. Carella might very well spit at him.

He wrestled with his problem, and he didn't sleep that night. He awoke on Saturday morning with the problem still fresh in his mind. He did not know why, but he wanted to see Steve Carella before he died. He wanted to see him and say hello, and maybe shake hands with him. Perhaps it was the Christmas season. Whatever it was, Danny took some coffee and a doughnut, and then he dressed carefully, putting on his good suit and a clean white shirt and choosing his tie carefully as well. He wanted to look respectable. He was going to the hospital on a respectable visit, and the entire unrespectability of his life seemed suddenly in very sharp focus. It seemed very important to him that he show his concern for Steve Carella, and it seemed equally important that Carella should respect him for it.

On the way to the hospital, he bought a box of candy. The candy gave him a good many moments of doubt. There would undoubtedly be cops at the hospital. Hadn't the desk sergeant said so? And wouldn't it look stupid for a stool pigeon to come carrying a box of candy? He almost threw the candy away, but he did not. When a man went to visit someone in the hospital, he brought something, something to say 'You're still with us, and you'll get well.' Danny Gimp was entering the polite, respectable world of civilized society, and so he would obey the rules of that society.

The sky beyond the hospital was very grey on that Saturday, 23 December. It looked like snow, and Danny thought fleetingly of the hundreds of people who were wishing for a white Christmas, and he felt a total sadness as he pushed through the hospital's revolving doors and entered the wide white entrance lobby. There was a big Christmas wreath on the wall opposite the reception desk, but there was nothing festive about the hospital itself. The girl behind the desk was polishing her nails. On a bench opposite the desk, an old man sat with his hat in his hands, glancing anxiously every few moments toward the Emergency Room down the corridor.

Danny took off his hat and walked to the desk. The girl did not look up. She painted her nails with the precision and skill of a Japanese dollmaker.

Danny cleared his throat. 'Miss?' he said.

'Yes,' the girl said, working the brush over her extended forefinger, covering the moon, splashing the oval with carmine brilliance.

'I'd like to see Steve Carella,' Danny said. 'Stephen Carella.'

'What is your name, sir?' the girl asked.

'Daniel Nelson,' he replied.

The girl put down the brush, held the fingers of the painted hand widespread, and reached for a typewritten sheet with the other hand. She reached for it automatically, without even looking for it. She put it down in front of her, studied it, and said, 'Your name's not on this list, sir.'

'What list?' Danny asked.

'Mr Carella is in a critical condition,' the girl said. 'We are admitting only members of his family and, because of the nature of the case, certain people from the police department. I'm sorry, sir.'

'Is he all right?' Danny asked.

The girl looked at him dispassionately. 'It's not usual to put a man on the critical list unless we feel his condition is critical,' she said.

'When . . . when will you know?' Danny asked.

'I have no way of telling, sir. He may rally, or he may not. I'm afraid it's out of our hands.'

'Is it all right if I wait?'

'Certainly, sir,' she said. 'You may sit on the bench there, if you like. It may be some time, you realize.'

'I realize,' Danny said. 'Thank you.'

He wondered why one of the few honest emotions he'd ever felt should be frustrated this way by a young chippie who was more interested in painting her nails than in life and death. He shrugged, blaming bureaucracy, and then went to sit on the bench alongside the old man. The old man turned to him almost instantly.

'My daughter cut her hand,' he said.

'Um?' Danny said.

'She was opening a can, and she cut her hand. Is that dangerous? A cut from a tin can, I mean?'

'I don't know,' Danny said.

'I heard it was. They're dressing the cut in there now. She was bleeding like a pig. I hope it isn't dangerous.'

'She'll be all right,' Danny said. 'Don't worry.'

'Well, I sure hope so. Did you come here to see somebody?'

'Yes,' Danny said.

'A friend?'

'Well,' Danny said. He half shrugged, and then began reading the list of ingredients on the candy box, wondering what lecithin was.

In a little while, the girl came out of the Emergency Room, her hand bandaged.

'Are you all right?' her father asked.

'Yes,' the girl said. 'They gave me a lollipop.'

Together, they went out of the hospital.

Alone, Danny Gimp sat on the bench, waiting.

Teddy Carella sat in the room with her husband, watching him. The blinds were drawn, but she could see his face clearly in the dimness, the mouth open, the eyes closed. Beside the bed, the plasma ran from an upturned bottle, slid through a tube, and entered Carella's arm. He lay without stirring, the blankets

136

pulled up over the jagged wounds in his chest. The wounds were dressed now, but they had leaked their blood, they had done their damage, and he lay pale and unmoving, as if death were already inside him.

No, she thought, *he won't die.*

Please God, please dear God, don't let this man die, please.

Her thoughts ran freely, and she didn't realize she was praying because her thoughts sounded only like thoughts to her, simple thoughts, the thoughts a girl thinks. But she was praying.

She was remembering how she'd met Carella, the day he'd come to the small office she'd worked for after they'd reported a burglary. She could remember exactly how he had come into the room, he and another man, a detective who was later transferred to another precinct, a detective whose face she could no longer remember. She had been concerned only with the face of Steve Carella that day. He had entered the office, and he was tall, and he walked erect, and he wore his clothes as if he were a high-priced men's fashion model rather than a cop. He had showed her his shield and introduced himself, and she had scribbled on a sheet of paper, explaining that she could neither hear nor speak, explaining that the receptionist was out, that she was hired as a typist, but that her employer would see him in a moment, as soon as she went to tell him the police were there. His face had registered mild surprise. When she rose from her desk and went to the boss's office, she could feel his eyes on her all the way.

She was not surprised when he asked her out.

She had seen interest in his eyes, and so the surprise was not in his asking, the surprise was that he could find her interesting at all. She supposed, of course, that there were men who would try anything once, just for kicks. Why not a girl who couldn't hear or talk? Might be interesting. She supposed, at first, that this was what had motivated Steve Carella, but after their first date, she knew this wasn't the case at all. He was not interested in her ears or her tongue. He was interested in the girl Teddy Franklin. He told her so, repeatedly. It took her a long while to believe it, even though she intuitively suspected its truth.

She had gone to bed with Carella because going to bed with him seemed the natural thing to do. He asked her to marry him often, but she never quite believed he really wanted her for his wife. And then one day, belief came, the way belief suddenly comes, and she realized he really and truly did want her for his wife. They were married on 19 August, and this was 23 December, and now he lay in a hospital bed, and it seemed he might die, it seemed possible he might die, the doctors had told her that her husband might die.

She did not concern herself with the unfairness of the situation. The situation was shockingly unfair, her husband should not have been shot, her husband should not now be fighting for his life on a hospital bed. The unfairness shrieked within her, but she did not concern herself with it, because what was done was done.

But he was good, and he was gentle, and he was her man, the only man in the world for her. There were those who held that any two people can make a go of it. If not one, then another. Throw them in bed together and things will work out all right. There's always another streetcar. Teddy did not believe this. Teddy did not believe that there was another man anywhere in the world who was as right for her as Steve Carella. Somehow, quite miraculously, he had been delivered to her doorstep, a gift, a wonderful gift.

She could not now believe he would be torn rudely from her. She could not believe it, she would not believe it. She had told him what she wanted for Christmas. She wanted him. She had said it earnestly, knowing he took it as jest, but she had meant every word of it. And now, her words were being hurled back into her face by a cruel wind. Because now she really wanted him for Christmas, now he was the only thing she really wanted for Christmas. Earlier, she had been secure when she asked for him, knowing she would certainly have him. But now, the security was gone, now there was left only a burning desire for her man to live. She would never again want anything more than Steve Carella.

And so, in the dimness of the room, she prayed, not knowing she was praying, and the words ran through her mind over and over and over again:

Let my husband live. Please let my husband live.

Detective-Lieutenant Peter Byrnes went down to the lobby at six fifteen that evening. He had been waiting in the corridor outside Carella's room all day long, hoping he could get to see him again. He had seen Carella only for a brief moment before Carella went unconscious again.

Carella had whispered a word, and the word was 'Gonzo'.

But Carella could say nothing more about the pusher, and so Byrnes still had only a flimsy description, a description he'd got from the three kids Carella had pinched in the car that day. No one else had heard of Gonzo, so how could Byrnes possibly pick him up? If Carella died . . .

He had put the thought out of his mind, sitting in the corridor. He called the precinct every half hour. And every half hour, he called home. The precinct had nothing to report. There were no leads to the new death of Dolores Faured. There were no leads to the old deaths of Aníbal and Maria Hernandez. There were no leads to Gonzo.

Things weren't much better at home. Larry was still in the process of shaking his sickness. The doctor had come again, but nothing seemed to displease Byrnes's son more. Byrnes wondered if he would ever be cured, and he wondered if they would ever find the man or men who were committing murder in his precinct. It was two days before Christmas, but Christmas would be a bleak time this year.

At six fifteen, he left the corridor and went down to the lobby. He stopped at the reception desk and asked the girl there if there was a decent eating place in the neighbourhood. She suggested a greasy spoon on Lafayette.

He was heading for the revolving doors when a voice called, 'Lieutenant?'

Byrnes turned. He didn't recognize the man at first. The man was small and thin, and he carried a box of candy under his arm, and he looked seedy, the way a normally seedy-looking person appears when he's trying to look dressed up. And then the face fell into place, and Byrnes said gruffly, 'Hello, Danny. What're you doing here?'

'I came to see Carella,' Danny said. He blinked and looked up at Byrnes.

'Yes?' said Byrnes, untouched.

'Yeah,' Danny said. 'How is he?'

'Bad,' Byrnes said. 'Look, Danny, you don't mind but I was on my way out to dinner. I'm kind of in a hurry.'

'Sure, sure,' Danny said.

Byrnes looked at him, and perhaps because it was almost Christmas, he added, 'You know how it is. This Gonzo character shooting Carella hasn't . . .'

'Who? Did you say Gonzo? Is he the one shot St— Detective Carella?'

'That's the way it looks,' Byrnes said.

'What are you telling me?' Danny asked. 'A punk kid like that? He took Steve Carella?'

'Why?' Byrnes said. He was interested now, but only because Danny had referred to Gonzo as if he knew him. 'What do you mean, a punk kid?'

'He can't be more than twenty, not the way I got it.'

'What do you know, Danny?'

'Well, like Ste— Well, Carella asked me to scout around on Gonzo, and I didn't come up with nothing. I mean, I scouted around because Ste . . .'

'For Christ's sake, call him Steve,' Byrnes said.

'Well, some cops are touchy about . . .'

'What have you got to say, Danny, goddamnit!'

'Even Steve don't like me calling him Steve,' Danny admitted, and then – seeing the look on Byrnes's face – rapidly went on. 'Nobody knew this Gonzo, you dig? So with me, it becomes a mathematical problem. How come these three kids coming to make a buy from this guy know him by Gonzo, and how come nobody on the scene knows him? It figures he ain't from the neighbourhood, am I right?'

'Go ahead,' Byrnes said, interested.

'Then I ask myself, if he ain't from the neighbourhood, how come he inherits the dead Hernandez's junk route? This don't figure. I mean, it looks like he at least knew Hernandez, don't it? And if he knew Hernandez, maybe he knew the sister, too. This is the way I was thinking, Lieutenant, putting together all the things Steve told me.'

'So what'd you get?'

'I got a guy who's a stranger in the neighbourhood, but who

maybe knew the Hernandezes. So I went to see the old lady, Mrs Hernandez. I talked to her, you know, fishing around, figuring this Gonzo was maybe a cousin or something, you know these Puerto Ricans – strong family ties.'

'*Is* he a cousin?'

'She don't make a cousin named Gonzo. She was talking true, too, because she knows me from the neighbourhood. Gonzo don't ring a bell.'

'I could have told you that, Danny. My men questioned Mrs Hernandez also.'

'But she tells me her son had a friend. He used to belong to the Sea Scouts, she says, and he used to go to these meetings up in Riverhead at a high school there. I check around, and I find out this is called the Junior Navals, a thing where some ex-Navy jerk got a bunch of kids together and slapped them in monkey suits so they could march around once a week. Only Hernandez don't go there to march. He goes there to push his junk. Anyway, the kid he knows there is called Dickie Collins.'

'How does this tie with Gonzo?'

'Well, listen,' Danny said. 'I start snooping around about this Dickie Collins kid. He used to live around here, moved a while ago, his old man got a job selling storm doors up in Riverhead, so the little extra dough enabled him to get the hell out of the neighbourhood. But Dickie's still got ties here, like that, you know? Comes back every now and then, and visits with the boys – including Aníbal Hernandez, the late. Met the sister a coupla times, too. Okay, so one night there's a card game. Small time, penny-ante stuff. This was only about two weeks ago, so it explains why there's nobody knows this Gonzo bit except four people, one of which is now dead. Luckily, I latched on to an alive one.'

'Spill it,' Byrnes said.

'There was four people in the game. A kid named Sam Di Luca, this kid Dickie Collins, Maria Hernandez, and an older guy from the neighbourhood.'

'Who was the older guy?'

'The Di Luca kid don't remember – and Maria Hernandez can't say any more. From what I could gather, they were shooting up that night, and this Di Luca's only sixteen, so he was probably blind. I got to explain this Di Luca kid, he calls himself Batman. That's his nickname. They all got nicknames, which is maybe why this Gonzo thing appealed.'

'Get to the point, Danny.'

'Okay. Sometime during the night, the four of them having a ball and playing cards, the older guy mentioned something about a cheap gunsel in the neighbourhood. Well, it turns out this kid Dickie Collins, he's never heard the word "gunsel". It's kind of a dead expression, you know, Lieutenant? I mean, hardly anybody but old-timers use it nowadays. Like "torpedo", you know? Out of fashion. So it's understandable, him being a snothouse kid, that he never heard it. But dig this. He says, "A gonzo? What the hell's a gonzo?" Now this broke up the joint. Maria fell off her chair, and the older guy was practically rolling on the floor, and Batman damn near wet his pants, it was so funny.'

'I see,' Byrnes said thoughtfully.

'So for the rest of the night, they kept calling him Gonzo. That's what this Batman tells me, anyway. But like there's only the four of them who know about it – just Batman, Maria, Dickie, and the older guy. And like Maria's pretty dead now, you know?'

'Dickie Collins is Gonzo,' Byrnes repeated blankly.

'Yeah. Batman, he forgot about the whole thing after that night. He was stinking drunk, anyway. But when I start asking about Gonzo, he remembers. The older guy, Christ alone knows who he is.'

'Dickie Collins,' Byrnes repeated.

'Sure. Lives in Riverhead now. One of the cheaper neighbourhoods there. You going to pick him up?'

'He shot Carella, didn't he?' Byrnes asked. He reached into his wallet and took out a ten-dollar bill. 'Here, Danny,' he said, offering the money.

Danny shook his head. 'No, Lieutenant, thanks.'

Byrnes stared at him unbelievingly.

'One thing you can do for me, though,' Danny said, somewhat embarrassed.

'What's that?'

'I'd like to go upstairs. I'd like to see Steve.'

Byrnes hesitated a moment. Then he walked to the desk and said, 'I'm Detective-Lieutenant Byrnes. This man is working on the case with us. I'd like him to go upstairs.'

'Yes, sir,' the girl said, and then she looked over toward Danny Gimp, who was smiling from ear to ear.

CHAPTER FIFTEEN

THEY caught Dickie Collins on Christmas Eve.

They caught him as he was coming out of church, where he had just lighted a candle for his dead grandmother.

They took him to the Squad Room of the 87th Precinct, and four detectives surrounded him there. One of the detectives was Peter Byrnes. The others were Havilland, Meyer, and Willis.

'What's your name?' Willis asked.

'Dickie Collins. Richard.'

'What aliases do you go by?' Havilland asked.

'None.'

'Ever own a gun?' Meyer asked.

'No. Never.'

'Know Aníbal Hernandez?' Byrnes asked.

'The name sounds familiar.'

'Did you know him, or didn't you?'

'Yeah, I knew him, I guess. I knew lots of kids in the neighbourhood.'

'When did you move?'

'Coupla months ago.'

'Why?'

'My old man got a new job. I go where he goes.'

'Did you want to move?'

'Makes no difference. I'm a free agent. I travel where I want to, no matter where I live. What's all the questions for? What did I do?'

'What were you doing on the night of 17 December?'

'How do I know? When the hell was that, anyway?'

'A week ago today.'

'I don't remember.'

'Were you with Hernandez?'

'I don't remember.'

'Start trying to remember.'

'No, I wasn't with Hernandez. What was that, a Saturday night?'

'It was a Sunday night.'

'No, I wasn't with him.'

'Where were you?'

'In church.'

'What?'

'I go to church every Sunday night. I light candles for my grandmother.'

'How long did you stay in church?'

'About an hour. I say a coupla prayers, too.'

'From what time to what time?'

'From about . . . from about ten to eleven.'

'And then what'd you do?'

'I drifted around.'

'Who saw you drifting?'

'Nobody. What do I need witnesses for? You trying to hang the Hernandez kill on me?'

'What makes you think he was killed?'

'He hung himself,' Collins said.

'Okay, but what made you call it a kill?'

'A suicide's a kill, ain't it?'

'Why should we try to hang a suicide on you?'

'How do I know? What else you got me in here for, if not that? You're asking questions about that night, ain't you? You're asking me if I knew Annabelle, ain't you?'

'You did know him.'

'Sure, I knew him.'

'From the neighbourhood or from the Sea Scouts?'

'What Sea Scouts?'

'In Riverhead.'

'Oh, you mean the Junior Navals. That ain't Sea Scouts. Yeah, yeah.'

'Where'd you know him from?'

144

'I used to say hello when I lived in the neighbourhood. Then, when I met him at the Navals, we got a little friendly.'

'Why'd you say you guessed you knew him? If you got friendly, then you knew him.'

'Okay, I knew him. Is that a crime?'

'Why'd you go to the Navals?'

'I didn't belong. I only went to watch the marching. I like to watch guys march.'

'You'll do a lot of marching where you're going,' Havilland said.

'Yeah, you got to send me there first, cop. I still ain't heard no charge. Are you booking or just looking?'

'You're a pusher, aren't you, Collins?'

'You're dreaming.'

'We've got three kids who made a buy from you. One is ready to identify you.'

'Yeah? What's his name?'

'Hemingway.'

'What're the other two called? Sinclair Lewis and William Faulkner?'

'You read a lot, Collins?'

'Enough.'

'This kid Hemingway doesn't read. He's a junkie. He bought a sixteenth of heroin from you on the afternoon of 20 December. One of our detectives nabbed him right after he made the buy.'

'So that's why I was being fol . . .' Collins cut himself short.

'What?'

'I didn't say nothing. If your Hemingway made a buy, he didn't get it from me.'

'He said he did. He said it came from you.'

'I don't know what a sixteenth of H looks like.'

'Did you know Hernandez was a junkie?'

'Yeah.'

'He ever shoot up with you?'

'No.'

'You never saw him shoot up?'

'No.'

'How do you know he was a junkie?'

'Word gets around.'

'Ever see him with any other junkies?'

'Sure.'

'Who?'

'I don't know their names.'

'Ever see him with a junkie named Larry Byrnes?' Byrnes asked.

Collins blinked.

'I said Larry Byrnes,' Byrnes repeated.

'Never heard of him,' Collins said.

'Think hard. He's my son.'

'No kidding? I didn't think cops had junkie sons.'

'Did you happen to see my son on the night of 17 December?'

'I wouldn't know your son from a hole in the wall.'

'How about the morning of 18 December?'

'I still don't know him, night or morning. How would I know him?'

'He knew Hernandez.'

'Lots of guys knew Hernandez. Hernandez was a pusher, didn't you know that?' Collins paused. 'Hell, he even pushed at the Navals.'

'We knew it. How'd you know it?'

'I seen him sell a couple of times.'

'To whom?'

'I don't remember. Listen, you think I know the names of every junkie in the neighbourhood? I never fooled with that crap myself.'

'You fooled with it on the twentieth, Collins. Two days after we found Hernandez dead, you were fooling with it. This Hemingway kid used to be one of Hernandez's customers.'

'Yeah? Maybe he bought that sixteenth from Hernandez's ghost, then.'

'He bought it from you.'

'You're gonna have a hell of a time proving that, cop.'

'Maybe not. We've had a man following you for the past few days.'

'Yeah?'

'Yeah.'

'So why didn't he pinch me? Listen, you find any stuff on me when you pulled me in? What am I here for, huh? I want a lawyer.'

'You're here on suspicion of murder,' Byrnes said.

'You mean . . .' Again, Collins stopped short.

'What, Collins?'

'Nothing. Hernandez hung himself. Just try pinning that one on me.'

'Hernandez died of an overdose.'

'Yeah? So he was careless.'

'Who put that rope around his neck, Collins?'

'Maybe your son did, Lieutenant. How about that?'

'How do you know my rank?'

'What?'

'If you don't know my son, and if you don't know anything about my son, how the hell do you know my rank?'

'One of your bulls called you Lieutenant. What do you think?'

'Nobody's called me anything since you got here, Collins. Now how about it?'

'I guessed. You look like you got leadership qualities, so I figured you were the boss. Okay?'

'Larry says he knows you,' Byrnes lied.

'Who's Larry?'

'My son.'

'Yeah? Lots of guys know me who I don't know. I'm popular.'

'Why? Because you're pushing junk?'

'Only thing I ever pushed was my sister's baby carriage. Get off that kick, cop. It leads nowhere.'

'Let's try another kick, Collins. Let's try cards.'

'What about them? Want to play some?'

'You ever play cards?'

'Sure, I do.'

'You ever play with a kid named Batman Di Luca?'

'Sure.'

'Who else was in that game?'

'Which game?'

'The night you played.'

147

'I played cards with Batman a lot. He can't play to save his ass. I always win.'

'What's a gunsel, Collins?'

'Huh?'

'A gunsel.'

'Oh.' Again, Collins blinked. 'A guy who's hired to wash somebody.'

'Pronounce it.'

'Gunsel. Say, what is this, an English class?'

'When did you find out what a gunsel was?'

'I always knew.'

'You found out that night of the card game, didn't you?'

'No, I didn't. I always knew.'

'Which night, Collins?'

'Huh?'

'You said you knew what a gunsel was before that night of the card game. Which night are we talking about?'

'The . . . the last time we played, I guess.'

'And when was that?'

'About . . . about two weeks ago.'

'And who played?'

'Me, Batman, and another guy.'

'Who was the third guy?'

'I don't remember.'

'Batman says you brought him down.'

'Me? No, it was Batman. I think he was a friend of Batman's.'

'He wasn't, and he isn't. Why are you protecting him, Collins?'

'I ain't protecting nobody. I don't even know who the guy was. Listen, I'd still like to know what you're driving at. You guys think –'

'Shut up!'

'Well, I got a right –'

'What happened on that night of the card game?'

'Nothing.'

'Who first mentioned the word "gunsel"?'

'I never heard it mentioned.'

'Then why'd you mispronounce it?'

'I didn't mispronounce it.'

'You pronounced it correctly?'

'Sure, I did.'

'How'd you pronounce it?'

'Gunsel.'

'When was this?'

'The night we ...' Collins stopped. '*Anytime* I pronounced it.'

'You said it wasn't mentioned on the night of the game.'

'I said I never heard it. Maybe it was mentioned, how should I know?'

'If it wasn't mentioned, where'd you get the nickname "Gonzo"?'

'Gonzo? Who's got a nickname Gonzo? Everybody calls me Dickie.'

'Except those three kids who came to make the buy from you.'

'Oh? Well, that explains it. You've got the wrong guy. You're looking for a Gonzo. My name is Dickie. Collins. Hey, maybe that's where you slipped up. Collins and Gonzo sound a little –'

'All right, let's cut the crap,' Havilland said sharply.

'Well, I ...'

'We know what happened at the card game. We know all about the gunsel routine and the way you goofed and called it "gonzo" and the way it brought down the house, and the way you were called Gonzo the rest of the night. Batman told us all about it, and Batman'll swear to it. We figure the rest like this, pal. We figure you used the Gonzo tag when you took over Hernandez's trade because you didn't figure it was wise to identify your own name with your identity as a pusher. Okay, so these kids were looking for Gonzo, and they found him, and one of them bought a sixteenth from you, and he'll swear to that, too. Now how about the rest?'

'What rest?'

'How about the cop you shot?'

'What?'

'How about that rope you put around Hernandez's neck?'

'What?'

'How about the slash job you did on Maria?'

'Listen, listen, I didn't –'

'How about shoving that old lady down the airshaft?'

'Me? Holy Jesus, I didn't do –'

'Which one did you do?'

'None of then! Holy Jesus, what do you take me for?'

'You shot that cop, Gonzo!'

'No, I didn't.'

'We know you did. He told us.'

'He told you nothing.'

'Who?'

'This cop, whoever you're talking about. He couldn't have said it was me because I had nothing to do with it.'

'You've got a lot to do with all of this, Gonzo.'

'Stop calling me Gonzo. My name's Dickie.'

'Okay, *Dickie*. Why'd you kill Hernandez? To get his two-bit business?'

'Don't be stupid!'

'Then why?' Byrnes shouted. 'To drag my son in on it? How'd Larry's fingerprints get on that syringe?'

'How do I know? What syringe?'

'The syringe found with Hernandez.'

'I didn't know there was one.'

'There was. How'd you swing it?'

'I didn't.'

'Were you trying to frame my son for this?'

'Stop harping on your son. Your son can go drop dead, for all I care.'

'Who's the man that calls me, Gonzo?'

'I didn't know anybody called you Gonzo.'

'Look, you rotten punk . . .'

'I don't know what you're talking about.'

'Somebody called to tell me about my son and that syringe. Somebody's got something on his mind. Was he the guy at that card game?'

'I don't know who that guy was.'

'The same guy who called me, isn't he?'

'I don't know who calls you.'

'The guy who helped you kill Hernandez, isn't it?'

'I didn't kill Hernandez.'

'And Maria, and the old lady . . .'

'I didn't kill anybody.'

'You killed a cop,' Willis snapped.

'Is he dead?' Collins asked.

The room was suddenly very quiet.

'What's wrong with that?' Collins said.

'You tell us, pal.'

'You told me a cop got shot. You didn't say he was dead.'

'No, we didn't.'

'Okay, so how was I supposed to know about the goddamn bull? You didn't say he was dead, only that he got shot.'

'We didn't say he was a bull, either,' Byrnes said.

'What?'

'We said a cop. What makes you think he's a detective?'

'I don't know, I just thought so. From the way you were talking.'

'His name is Steve Carella,' Willis said. 'You shot him on Friday, Collins, and he's still fighting for his life. He *told* us you shot him. Why don't you tell us the rest of it, and make it easy for yourself?'

'There's nothing to tell. I'm clean. If your cop dies, you ain't got a thing on me. I ain't got a gun, and I wasn't carrying no junk. So do me something.'

'We're gonna do you a lot, pal,' Havilland said. 'In about three seconds flat, I'm gonna beat the crap out of you.'

'Go ahead. See what that gets you. I ain't involved in none of this. Your cop is crazy. I didn't shoot him, and I got nothing to do with Hernandez, either. You going to build a friendship at the Junior Navals into a federal case?'

'No,' Willis said, 'but we're going to build your footprint into a murder case, that's for sure.'

'My *what*?'

'The footprint we found near Carella's body,' Willis lied. 'We're going to check it against every pair of shoes you own. If it matches up, you're –'

'We were standing on stone!' Collins shouted.

And that was it.

He blinked, realizing it was too late to turn back now, realizing they had him cold. 'Okay,' he said, 'I shot him. But only because he was going to take me in. I didn't want to get tied in with this other stuff. I had nothing to do with killing Hernandez or his sister. Nothing. And I never saw that old lady in my life.'

'Who killed them?' Byrnes asked.

Collins was silent for a moment.

'Douglas Patt,' he said at last.

Willis was already starting for his coat. 'No,' Byrnes called, 'I want him. What's his address, Collins?'

CHAPTER SIXTEEN

IT was very cold up on the roof, colder perhaps than any place in the city. The wind swept around the chimney pots and ate into a man's bones. You could see the entire city almost from up there on the roof, the lights winking, a city of secrets, little secrets.

He stood for a moment and looked out past the rooftops, and he wondered how everything could have gone so wrong. The plan seemed like such a good one, and yet it had gone wrong. *Too many people*, he thought. Whenever there are too many people, things go wrong.

He sighed and turned his back to the cutting wind that whipped the clothes lines and the fragile panes of glass in the walls of the buildings. He felt very tired, and somehow very lonely. It shouldn't have worked out this way. A plan so good should have worked out better. Despondently, he walked to the pigeon coop. He took a key from his pocket and unlocked the door, hanging the lock back on the latch. He stepped into the coop, and the pigeons – alarmed for a moment – beat their wings and then resolved their private fears and settled down again.

He saw the female fantail almost instantly.

She lay on the floor of the coop, and he knew at once that she was dead.

Gently, he bent down and picked her up, and he held her on

his widespread hands, staring at her, as if staring would bring her back to life.

Everything seemed suddenly too much to bear. Everything seemed to have been leading to this ultimate, crushing defeat: the death of his fantail. He kept watching the bird, aware that his hands were trembling, but unable to stop them. He went out of the coop then, still holding the bird in his hands. He walked across the roof, and he sat with his back to one of the chimney pots. He put the bird down gently at his feet, and then – as if his hands were too idle now that they were empty – he picked up a loose brick and turned it over and over in his hands, like a potter working with wet clay. He was turning the brick, slowly, slowly, when the man came up on to the roof.

The man looked around for a moment and then walked directly to where he was sitting.

'Douglas Patt?' the man asked.

'Yes?' he answered. He looked up into the man's eyes. The eyes were very hard. The man stood with his shoulders hunched against the wind, his hands in his pockets.

'I'm Lieutenant Byrnes,' the man said.

'Oh,' Patt answered.

They looked at each other silently for a long time. Patt made no motion to rise. Slowly, he kept turning the brick over in his hands, the dead bird at his feet.

'How did you get to me?' he asked at last.

'Dickie Collins,' Byrnes said.

'Mmm,' Patt said. He didn't seem to care very much. He didn't seem at all interested in how the police had found him. 'I figured he would be a weak link if you got on to him.' Patt shook his head. 'Too many people,' he said. He looked down at the bird. He gripped the brick more tightly in one hand.

'What'd you hope to get out of this, Patt?' Byrne asked.

'Me?' Patt said. He made a motion to rise, and Byrnes moved quickly and effortlessly, so that by the time Patt was squatting on his haunches he was looking into the level muzzle of Byrnes's pistol. But Patt seemed not to notice the gun. He seemed intent only on studying the dead bird at his feet. He moved the bird with one hand, holding the brick in the other hand. 'Me? What did I want out of this? A chance, Lieutenant. Big time, Lieutenant.'

'How?'

'This kid, Gonzo – you know about the Gonzo, don't you? Silly damn thing, isn't it? But sort of weird – this kid, Gonzo, he came to me and said, "How do you like that? Annabelle tells me he's got a junkie friend whose old man runs the dicks at the 87th." That's what Gonzo said to me, Lieutenant.'

Byrnes watched him. Patt had lifted the brick slowly, and now he brought it down almost gently, but with a gentle force, smashing it against the body of the dead pigeon. He brought back the brick again, and again he hit the bird with it. There was blood on the brick now, and feathers. He brought it back unconsciously, and then down again, almost as if he were unaware of what he was doing to the bird.

'I figured this was it, Lieutenant. I figured I'd get your son into a set-up that looked pretty bad, and then I'd come to you, Lieutenant, and lay my cards on the table and say, "This is how it stands, Lieutenant. Your son's story gets blabbed all over the newspapers unless I get your cooperation." I had your son rigged for a murder rap, Lieutenant. I was sure you'd cooperate.'

He kept pounding with the brick. Byrnes pulled his eyes away from the disintegrating bird.

'What kind of cooperation did you expect?'

'I push,' Patt said. 'But I'm afraid. I could really expand if I didn't have to be afraid all the time. I didn't want to take a fall. I wanted you to help. I wanted hands off from you or any of your dicks. I wanted to be free to roam the precinct and push wherever I wanted to, without being afraid of getting pinched. That's what I wanted, Lieutenant.'

'You'd never have got it,' Byrnes said. 'Not from me, and not from any cop.'

'Maybe not from you. But, oh, it was sweet, Lieutenant. I sold this little Annabelle jerk a bill of goods. I told him all I wanted was a syringe with your son's prints on it. He dragged your son in and gave him a free fix, and then he switched syringes before your son left that night. I was waiting. When

154

your son took off, I went in to see Annabelle. He was nodding, half blind. I loaded a syringe with enough H to knock the top of his head off. He didn't even know I was injecting it. Then I took your son's syringe out of Annabelle's pocket, and I laid it on the cot beside him.'

'Why the rope?' Byrnes asked.

Patt kept hitting the bird, pulverizing it with the brick, spewing feathers and blood on to the tar of the roof. 'That was an afterthought. It occurred to me – Jesus, suppose they think it is a suicide? Or suppose they think it was just an accidental overdose? Where does that leave my murder frame? So I put the rope around Annabelle's neck. I figured the police would be smart enough to know it was tied there after he was killed. I wanted them to know it was homicide, because I was measuring your son for the rap. Your son was my bargaining tool, Lieutenant. My bargaining tool for a free precinct.'

'A free precinct,' Byrnes repeated.

'Mmm, yes,' Patt said. 'But it didn't work out, did it? And then Maria, and the old woman – how do these things get so complicated?'

He stopped pounding and looked down at the tar suddenly. The bird was a crushed mass of bloody pulp and feathers. The brick was stained with blood, as were Patt's hands. He looked at the pigeon, and then he looked at the brick and his hands as if he were seeing them for the first time. And then, quite suddenly, he began sobbing.

'You'd better come with me,' Byrnes said gently.

They booked him at the 87th. They charged him with the murder of three people. And after he'd been booked, Byrnes went up to his office, and he stood looking out over the park, and then he saw the clock in the park tower, and the clock told him it was five minutes to midnight.

Five minutes to Christmas.

He went to his telephone.

'Yes?' the desk sergeant said.

'This is the Lieutenant,' Byrnes said. 'Can I have a line, please?'

'Yes, sir.'

155

He waited for his dial tone, and then he dialled his Calm's Point number, and Harriet answered the phone.

'Hello, Harriet,' he said.

'Hello, Peter.'

'How is he?'

'I think he's going to be all right,' she said.

'He's better?'

'Better than he was, Peter. He doesn't seem ... he hasn't been vomiting or fidgeting or behaving like a wild man. I think he's licked it physically, Peter. The rest is up to him.'

'Yes,' Byrnes said. 'Is he awake?'

'Yes, he is.'

'May I talk to him?'

'Certainly, darling.'

'Harriet?'

'Yes?'

'I know I've been chasing around, but I wanted you to know ... I mean, all this running around these past few days ...'

'Peter,' she said gently, 'I married a cop.'

'I know you did. I'm grateful for it. Merry Christmas, Harriet.'

'Come home as soon as you can, darling. I'll get Larry.'

Byrnes waited. In a little while, his son came to the phone.

'Dad?'

'Hello, Larry. How are you feeling?'

'Much better, Dad.'

'Good, good.'

There was a long silence.

'Dad?'

'Yes?'

'I'm sorry for the way ... for, you know, what I've done. It's going to be different.'

'A lot of things are going to be different, Larry,' Byrnes promised.

'Will you be coming home soon?'

'Well, I wanted to wind up ...' Byrnes stopped. 'Yes, I'll be home very soon. I want to stop off at the hospital, and then I'll be right home.'

'We'll wait up, Dad.'

'Fine, I'd like that.' Byrnes paused. 'You really feel all right, Larry?'

'Well, I'm getting there,' Larry said, and Byrnes thought he detected a smile in his son's voice.

'Good. Merry Christmas, son.'

'We'll be waiting.'

Byrnes hung up and then put on his overcoat. He was suddenly feeling quite good about everything. They had caught Patt, and they had caught Collins, and his son would be all right, he was sure his son would be all right, and now there remained only Carella, and he was sure Carella would pull through, too. Damnit, you can't shoot a good cop and expect him to die! Not a cop like Carella!

He walked all the way to the hospital. The temperature was dipping close to zero, but he walked all the way, and he shouted, 'Merry Christmas!' to a pair of drunks who passed him. When he reached the hospital, his face was tingling, and he was out of breath, but he was more sure than ever before that everything would work out all right.

He took the elevator up to the eighth floor, and the doors slid open and he stepped into the corridor. It took a moment to orient himself and then he started off toward Carella's room, and it took another moment for the new feeling to attack him. For here in the cool antiseptic sterility of the hospital, he was no longer certain about Steve Carella. Here he had his first doubts, and his step slowed as he approached the room.

He saw Teddy then.

At first she was only a small figure at the end of the corridor, and then she walked closer and he watched her. Her hands were wrung together at her waist, and her head was bent, and Byrnes watched her and felt a new dread, a dread that attacked his stomach and his mind. There was defeat in the curve of her body, defeat in the droop of her head.

Carella, he thought. *Oh God, Steve, no ...*

He rushed to her, and she looked up at him, and her face was streaked with tears, and when he saw the tears on the face of Steve Carella's wife, he was suddenly barren inside, barren and cold, and he wanted to break from her and run down the corridor, break from her and escape the pain in her eyes.

157

And then he saw her mouth.

And it was curious, because she was smiling. She was smiling and the shock of seeing that smile opened his eyes wide. The tears coursed down her face, but they ran past a beaming smile, and he took her shoulders and he spoke very clearly and very distinctly and he said, 'Steve? Is he all right?'

She read the words on his mouth, and then she nodded, a small nod at first, and then an exaggerated delirious nod, and she threw herself into Byrnes's arms, and Byrnes held her close to him, feeling for all the word as if she were his daughter, surprised to find tears on his own face.

Outside the hospital, the church bells tolled.

It was Christmas Day, and all was right with the world.

MORE ABOUT PENGUINS
AND PELICANS

Penguinews, which appears every month, contains details of all the new books issued by Penguins as they are published. From time to time it is supplemented by *Penguins in Print*, which is our complete list of almost 5,000 titles.

A specimen copy of *Penguinews* will be sent to you free on request. Please write to Dept EP, Penguin Books Ltd, Harmondsworth, Middlesex, for your copy.

In the U.S.A.: For a complete list of books available from Penguins in the United States write to Dept CS, Penguin Books, 625 Madison Avenue, New York, New York 10022.

In Canada: For a complete list of books available from Penguins in Canada write to Penguin Books Canada Ltd, 2801 John Street, Markham, Ontario L3R 1B4.